A
Harlequin
Romance

OTHER
Harlequin Romances
by FLORA KIDD

THE LEGEND OF
THE SWANS

by

FLORA KIDD

HARLEQUIN BOOKS   TORONTO
WINNIPEG

Original hard cover edition published in 1973
by Mills & Boon Limited.

© Flora Kidd 1973

SBN 373-01774-X

Harlequin edition published April 1974

Printed in Canada

1774

CHAPTER ONE

IT was seven-thirty in the morning. Shafts of yellow sunlight, filtering through fine net curtains, touched the pale face of the young woman who was asleep in the bed, and brought to life a faint sparkle of red in the ruffled mass of curling brown hair which was spread across the pillow.

The bell of the alarm clock on the bedside table began to sound. It was a pleasant mellifluous chiming, designed to make waking up a joy. It stopped and music took its place, filling the room with gay noise composed to make any sleeper want to bound out of bed to greet the April morning happily.

Long brown eyelashes, which were spread out on the pale cheeks, fluttered and were raised to reveal the gleam of green-shot golden eyes. A long slim arm appeared from under the bedclothes, stretched out and the music was turned off. With a groan the young woman turned in bed and buried her head into the plump soft pillow.

The door of the room, which was partially open, swayed slightly as a blue Persian kitten sidled through it. The kitten paused in the doorway, his whiskers quivering. Suddenly he yawned widely, revealing a tiny pink tongue and sharp white teeth. Gathering himself together, he sprang forward and landed on the bed. Purring loudly, he began to knead the bedclothes with his padded paws. The expression on his face was ecstatic, the eyes half-closed, the black line of the mouth turned upwards at the corners.

Georgina Marriott, known to her friends and relatives as Gina, opened her eyes properly this time, looked at the kitten and then at the clock. Had she imagined hearing the alarm? She peered at it. Seven-thirty-five. April the twelfth. Memory came surging back and she groaned again, not wishing to face up to it, trying to escape from the knowledge that Oliver was dead and that she was not married. Once more she buried her head in the pillow as if by doing so she could forget, but the kitten continued with his kneading and his purring, knowing that if he did so his owner would be forced to wake up properly.

Listening to Blue's familiar purring, Gina kept her eyes stubbornly closed. In the back of her mind she knew that she had set the alarm purposely last night to wake her early because today she was going for an interview for a job and she wanted to spend the morning preparing her clothes so that she would look her best.

But, as on every morning since she had received the news that Oliver Fox, her fiancé, had been killed in a car crash, inertia claimed her. Of what use was it to get up and dress, to put on an act, to attempt to be interested in a job, when all she wanted was to die?

The door was pushed open more widely and a tall blonde girl, dressed in a blatant purple woollen suit which she wore with a white high-necked sweater, entered the room carefully carrying a cup and saucer. Gilt bracelets jangled on her wrists, gilt chains swung between her firm breasts and gilt ear-rings glinted wickedly amongst her blonde curls. An expression of concern marked her normally cheerful face as she glanced at the recumbent figure in the bed.

'Wakey, wakey, Gina love. Here's a nice cup of tea. Remember you're going for that interview. Make the most of yourself. Why not wear that new suit, the wheat-coloured one?'

'I'm not going,' mumbled Gina from the depths of the pillow.

Lynette Brown, affectionately known as Birdie on account of her first name, looked troubled.

'But, Gina, it'll do you good to go out. Remember what Dr Lambert said? You must have a change. Go away from here. Make a complete break with the hospital and everything associated with Oliver. Only that way will you recover from the shock quickly.'

6

Still Gina did not move. Only the back of her ruffled head was on show.

'Birdie, will you please do me a favour?' she asked in a muffled voice.

'Of course I will, love,' said the generous kindly Birdie.

'Go to work now,' said Gina flatly.

Exasperation took the place of tender anxiety on Birdie's face.

'Oh, Gina, what am I going to do with you?' she exclaimed.

'You don't have to do anything,' replied Gina. 'I've got to work this out by myself. Thanks for the tea. Now, please leave me alone.'

'All right. But I still think you should go for the interview. Don't forget I'm giving a party tonight for Pam Harwood.'

Gina groaned, 'Must you?'

'Yes, I must. I promised. And remember it's Mrs Chadwick's day for cleaning the flat, so you'll have to get up some time.'

'Leave the front door unlocked so that she can get in,' muttered Gina. 'G'bye.'

' 'Bye,' replied Birdie, and shrugging her shoulders helplessly she left the room.

Gina did not move. On the bedside table the tea grew cold. Blue, the kitten, stopped kneading, and curling round and round several times to make a warm spot, he settled down to have a snooze.

The minutes ticked away. The shafts of sunlight grew stronger and their angle altered slightly. The outer door of the flat opened and a small woman entered the hallway, removed her coat and hung it in a cupboard. She went into the kitchenette and clucked her tongue at the pile of dishes there. Then, humming to herself, she began to run water into the sink.

In the bedroom all was quiet except for the purring of the dozing kitten. Suddenly the telephone on the bedside

7

table rang persistently. The kitten sat up, eyes wide, ears twitching. The telephone continued to ring. Gina moaned, stretched out an arm, lifted the receiver and, with her eyes still closed, murmured sleepily into the mouthpiece.

'Hello.'

'Did I wake you up?'

The question was asked by a masculine voice with a lazy lilt to it. The voice was completely strange to Gina. Her eyes flew open and she sat up straight in bed.

'Who's speaking?' she asked.

'Will Fox. I almost became your brother-in-law. I'd like to come and see you.'

The voice was crisp now, autocratic in tone.

'Oh—er—Mr Fox,' stuttered Gina, caught with her defences down. 'That's nice of you, but I'm sorry, I'm not receiving visitors yet. I haven't been very well and...'

'That's too bad,' the voice interrupted her, rudely, Gina thought. 'I won't be this way again and I'd like to see the girl Noll chose to be his mate. Also I've something to suggest which might be of interest to you. Sure you won't change your mind about inviting me round?'

'Mr Fox——' Gina began.

'Captain,' he corrected curtly.

'Then, Captain Fox, I've said I'm sorry I can't see you,' she said in a cool clear voice. 'Oliver's death was a great shock to me. The doctor recommended rest and then a complete change. He said I was to have nothing to do with anything or anyone connected with Oliver.' That wasn't entirely true, but it was all she could think of on the spur of the moment. 'Besides,' she added, 'I don't think you would gain anything by meeting me at present.'

There was silence at the other end of the line. She was just thinking that he had hung up or that they had been cut off, when he spoke again, softly and yet clearly, almost as if he were beside her in the room and was whispering into her ear.

'I think you should let me be the judge of that,' he said.

8

'I don't know what you mean,' she stammered.

'I mean I prefer to be the one who decides whether I shall gain anything by meeting you.' He was crisp again. 'I could be at your flat in a few minutes.'

'Oh no, Mr—I mean, Captain Fox, I couldn't possibly be ready to meet you. I don't want you to come here. I want to be left alone, I've no wish to see anyone.'

She became suddenly aware that the ringing tone was sounding in her ear. He'd hung up on her.

Gina set the receiver back on its rest and leaned against the pillows. Two patches of brilliant colour glowed in her cheeks, fantastic blobs of red on her pale cheeks. When she glanced downwards she saw her breast was rising and falling rapidly as her heart beat faster than normally.

Captain Fox. Captain William Fox. Captain of what? She tried to recall what Oliver had told her about his elder brother, but her mind was foggy on the subject. She could remember sending a wedding invitation to him, against Oliver's wishes. The address had been somewhere in the Highlands of Scotland. He had replied, but she could not remember whether he had accepted or declined the invitation.

Her forgetfulness acted as a spur. Before she realised it she was out of bed and standing at her dressing table, searching through the papers in the top drawer. Small and slender, but with softly-rounded seductive curves, her legs shapely below the hem of her short diaphanous nightgown, her brown hair cascading about her shoulders, she looked much younger than her twenty-three years and gave an initial impression of someone who was helpless and vulnerable.

The replies to the wedding invitations were not where she expected them to be. Then she remembered they were in a folder in the drawer of the bedside table. She padded over the shaggy orange carpet, gently chastising Blue, who had left the bed and was rubbing himself against her bare legs.

She was leafing through the correspondence in the buff folder when there was a knock on the door. It struck Gina that Mrs Chadwick was extraordinarily noisy that morning, then she called to her to come in.

Behind her the door opened and closed just as the letter from William Fox appeared. The name leapt out from the paper, bold and authoritative-looking, just as Blue hissed and spat, and jumped up on to the bedside table, knocking the cup of cold tea over and scattering letters, cup and saucer to the floor.

'Naughty Blue!' scolded Gina, lifting the kitten from the floor. 'It's only Mrs C.'

'No, it isn't,' said the masculine voice she had heard only a short time ago over the phone. 'It's me.'

Gina whirled round. Above the kitten's blue fur her face was white, her green-gold eyes were shadowed, deeply sunk in their sockets, but they blazed with indignation as they met those of the man who leaned against the closed door of her room.

'Who let you in?' she demanded.

Big-shouldered and slim-hipped, he was built like a heavyweight boxer. His nose looked as if it had once been broken and re-set and a white, wicked-looking scar, which could have been caused by a knife wound, angled across one lean cheek. He wasn't handsome with a suave regularity of feature, as Oliver had been, but neither was he ugly. His face suggested a rugged rock-like personality and she guessed he could be rough when he wanted.

'Mrs Chadwick did,' he replied with an urbanity which contradicted his looks. His light blue eyes, deep-set under thick dark eyebrows, were busy taking in her appearance, making her feel very conscious of the brevity of her gown. She hugged Blue close to her as if for protection from that curious gaze, but the kitten objected to being detained, struggled free and, jumping down, went to hide under the bed.

'She had no right! How dare you come in here! Go

away!' The words came out with the rapidity of machine-gun fire as Gina, furious by now, clasped her arms across her bosom.

He grinned and his face changed miraculously. She was looking at a mischievous boy who would never take no for an answer.

'Surprise tactics have always been my speciality,' he said calmly. 'I told her I was a close relative of yours and that I'd come to see you to commiserate with you in your loss. We had quite a little chat together about you. You've sunk pretty low in her estimation.'

Gina was surprised.

'Oh! Why?'

'You've been lying in bed until all hours, opting out.'

Gina discovered she was shaking. How dared Mrs Chadwick discuss her with this rude man! She tried to object, only to find she was so angry she couldn't speak. So she just stood there by the bed, pale and trembling, as her unwanted visitor strode over to the dressing table and picked up the photograph of Oliver. He stared at it for a moment and then swung round to look at her.

'And how long have you been wallowing in self-pity?' he asked in easy conversational tones, as he replaced the photograph.

Her body stiffened, her head came up and her eyes sparkled dangerously.

'You may not have realised it, Captain Fox, but the days of keeping a stiff upper lip are over. None of us have to pretend we're not hurt any more,' she retorted. 'The man I loved was killed two days before our wedding day. Is it any wonder I'm shocked and sorry for myself?'

In one stride he was standing over her, his light eyes cold, his wide expressive mouth curling into a sneer.

'It isn't any wonder Mrs Chadwick is disappointed in you,' he jeered. 'No spunk, she said.' His glance shifted to the bedside table and he reached out a hand to pick up the bottle of sleeping pills which had been recommended by Dr

11

Lambert. He read the label and his scornful gaze came back to hers. 'Is this the drug you use to help you to escape from reality?' he demanded sternly.

Anger was now an insistent throb, beating through her mind, thrusting aside the torpidity which had claimed her body and mind for the past week. She longed to strike at this man who had invaded her room. Why, even Oliver had never been in this room and had never seen her in such a dishevelled state, and she had been engaged to marry him!

'I don't take drugs,' she flung at him icily. Hands clenched by her sides, shoulders back, she stood up straight, no longer concerned about how she looked. 'Now, will you please go before I call the police?'

The sneer faded from his face and was replaced by the mischievous grin. He folded his arms across his chest and rocked back and forth on his heels.

'Why do you want to call them?' he asked mildly.

'You've invaded my privacy and I wish to dress,' she retorted haughtily.

'Oh, is that all that's bothering you?' he murmured, letting his glance rove again. His gaze come back to hers. Devilment was in his eyes now, blue and twinkling, dancing between soot-black lashes. 'Go ahead. I can turn my back. It won't be the first time I've been present in a woman's room when she's not dressed.'

'That I can believe,' she hissed, and reached blindly for the telephone receiver. Her hand never reached it because he caught and held her slim fingers in his much bigger hand. Furiously she tried to twist them free, but shock and unhappiness had weakened her and she was no match for his superior strength. Suddenly very near to tears, she found herself leaning against him helplessly, rather appalled at her own violent behaviour.

'I'll go from the room on one condition,' he offered softly, and she felt his breath stirring her hair.

'Yes?' she whispered. 'What is it?'

'If you'll come into the other room when you're dressed

and listen to a suggestion I have to make to you.'

The roughness had gone from his voice. It was kind, almost tender. She lifted heavy eyelids and gazed up at his rock-like jaw. It was difficult to believe that he was Oliver's brother. Oliver's hands had never grasped hers bruisingly, like this. Oliver's mouth had been chiselled, almost perfect in shape. Above the rock-like jaw this man's mouth was wide and curving and the lower lip was full and sensual.

'Well? Do you agree?' he asked.

Her glance went past his mouth, past the jutting broken nose to his eyes. They were not the soft pansy blue of Oliver's, but the cold clear blue of ice-girt seas, and beyond them the craggy, lined forehead was framed by close-clinging slightly curly hair, several shades darker than Oliver's had been, almost black.

'I agree,' she submitted, thinking she had no alternative but to agree when held like this.

'That's better.'

He released her and left the room. Alone, Gina took several deep breaths, examined closely the marks left by his fingers on her wrist. Then she went over to her wardrobe and began to take out the clothes she intended to wear.

She guessed that Oliver had told her very little about his elder brother because their relationship had not been a very close one. After all, there had been a difference of eight years in their ages. Oliver had just celebrated his twenty-seventh birthday before he was killed, which meant that the big brute in the next room was thirty-five. He looked every day of it too, thought Gina waspishly, and then she wondered at her own strong feelings. She had not felt any strong emotion for days.

Having chosen a pair of sleek wheat-coloured pants and a matching angora sweater to wear, she went off to the bathroom. For fifteen minutes she soaked herself in the perfumed water. Then she dried herself in a leisurely fashion, trying all the time to recall anything that Oliver might have told her about his brother.

13

If she remembered rightly Oliver's father had been killed in some sort of accident when serving with the British Army. William had been seventeen at the time and had followed in his family's tradition by joining the Army, much against his mother's wishes.

His mother had married again, choosing as her second husband a man who followed a much more peaceful profession, that of the law. When her younger son had shown an interest in medicine as a career, she had encouraged him. Gina had met Oliver and William's mother, now Mrs Ann Simpson, and she had the utmost admiration for her calm well-organised attitude to life and her active participation in the various voluntary associations in the town of Leamington, where she lived.

Oliver had studied medicine at Birmingham University, and it was while he was in his fifth and final year there and she was in her third and final year at the local domestic science college that they had met.

The only daughter of fairly wealthy parents, Gina did not really have to work, but she had always been interested in cooking and in household management, so her parents had thought the training would be useful to her.

When she had qualified, with honours in institutional management, she had gone to work in the hospital where Oliver had been working as a house surgeon. It was at that time she had left her parents' home and had moved into a mews flat, in the still-elegant suburb of Edgbaston, which she shared with her old school friend Birdie. Six months later she and Oliver had become engaged.

Quickly, plans had gone ahead for a wedding. It was to have been the spring wedding of the year, between Oliver, son of the late Lt.-Colonel Geoffrey Fox and Mrs Ann Simpson of Leamington, and Georgina, daughter of Mr and Mrs David Marriott of Henley-in-Arden. Birdie was to have been the only bridesmaid and John Oldham was to have been best man. They were to have gone to Malta for their honeymoon, returning to live in a pleasant modern

14

detached house in one of the better suburbs of Birmingham.

Everything had been ready. She had given up her job at the hospital to spend the last week of her life as a single woman preparing herself mentally and physically for marriage. Although there had been moments, terrifying moments, when she had wanted escape from her commitment to Oliver and run as far away as possible, she had never admitted those moments to anyone.

Then the blow had fallen. Returning by car from a Rugby Union game, which he had gone to see at Twickenham with some friends as his last fling as a bachelor, Oliver had been killed in one of the multiple crashes caused by fog on the motorway, and the dream of the perfect marriage had been shattered.

Suddenly the door of the bedroom was hit by the flat of someone's hand. It trembled and Gina spun round from the dressing-table mirror, fully expecting William Fox to march in. But the door didn't open. He merely called through it.

'Hurry up. I haven't got all day to waste waiting for you to titivate.'

Grimacing at the door, Gina controlled a desire to throw something at it, and with an effort she sang out sweetly,

'Coming!'

She turned back to the mirror, finished applying her lipstick, tilted her head this way and that to survey the way she had arranged her hair, high on her head in a smooth chignon with a few corkscrew curls dangling tantalisingly in front of her ears. Then, satisfied that she looked cool and sophisticated, she opened the door, went down the passage and made what she hoped was a stunning entrance into the living room.

The effort was wasted. The living room was empty. From the kitchenette came the most delicious smell of bacon and eggs cooking mingled with the aroma of percolating coffee.

Gina's stomach gurgled noisily. She hadn't eaten properly for days and now she felt ravenously hungry. Surely Mrs Chadwick wasn't cooking breakfast? She wasn't paid to cook, just to clean.

Quickly Gina crossed the room to the door leading to the kitchen. She looked round it. William Fox, seeming much bigger because of the smallness of the room, was standing by the cooker. His shabby tweed jacket was off, the collar of his checked Viyella shirt was undone and its tail was half in and half out of the waistband of his thick Army pants. His tie was dangling over the back of one of the kitchen chairs.

'What do you think you're doing?' demanded Gina in her most supercilious tones.

He glanced round.

'Cooking breakfast. Want some?' he asked genially. 'I've set a place for you, working on the theory that the smell of someone else's bacon cooking always makes me feel hungry and so the same might apply to you.'

He opened the oven door, took out two plates which had been warming, and expertly scooped bacon and eggs from the frying pan on to them.

'You've no right——' Gina started, then changed her mind and exclaimed, 'Where's Mrs Chadwick?'

'I sent her home. Told her to come back on Monday. I hope you don't mind.'

'Mind!' Gina discovered she was shrieking in a most unbecoming shrewish fashion. 'Of course I mind. She hasn't finished cleaning yet, and she won't be able to come on Monday because she works for someone else then.'

'Well, you're doing nothing these days, so it won't take you long to make the beds, vacuum and flutter a duster about,' he replied easily, setting the plates on the table. 'There you are. Eat up,' he ordered. 'How do you like your coffee, black or white?'

'I don't. I prefer tea,' she seethed.

'Ah well, *chacun à son gout*. You'll have to make the tea yourself.'

He sat down on one of the spindly kitchen chairs and

Gina wished quite viciously that it would disintegrate beneath his weight and land him on the floor.

'Come on, George,' he invited. 'Sit down and be friendly.'

She sat down and tried not to be interested in the food. He cocked a dark eyebrow at her, pursed his lips and gave a wolf whistle.

'My mother told me you were beautiful,' he murmured, 'but I didn't believe her because she'd always had a tendency to exaggerate about anything connected with Noll. He was her blue-eyed boy and he always had to have the best of everything, even if in actual fact, he didn't always choose the best. This time, however, I'm willing to concede she's right. He really picked a winner in you when it came to looks. You are beautiful, or you will be when you've matured a bit more. That outfit you're wearing is the latest, I suppose.' His grin flickered wickedly. 'I must say I prefer you in a nightie. Are you sure you won't have some coffee?'

'Captain Fox——' began Gina, speaking through gritted teeth.

'I shan't object if you call me Will, George,' he put in generously.

'My name isn't George!' she flared, goaded beyond endurance and stamping her foot on the floor.

'Tut, tut, what a temper,' he reproved her. 'You'll feel much better when you've eaten. Then we'll talk for a while, then we'll go out. I thought we'd go for a drive somewhere. I'd like to go to Stratford. I've never been there. Later we could have dinner together at some country pub. By then I think we'll know each other pretty well. Don't you, George?'

'I've no wish to know you any better,' she replied coolly.

Picking up her knife and fork, she began to attack the food which she could resist no longer. He stared at her bent head with narrowed observant eyes, picked up the coffee pot and poured coffee into the second cup. He pushed the cup and saucer across to her.

'Georgina's a heck of a name,' he remarked. 'What did Noll call you?'

'If by Noll you mean Oliver, he called me Gina like everyone else does,' she replied haughtily.

He made a face at her.

'I prefer George,' he said.

'I don't really care what you prefer since I have no desire to be acquainted with you any further,' she said silkily, wondering how she could get rid of him.

'You may not have any desire to be, but you're going to be. I need a woman.'

Her head came up in shocked reaction to this blatant statement and he grinned at her.

'One who can cook for large numbers of people and knows how to cater for them,' he continued easily, although his eyes twinkled with devilment again in acknowledgement of her shocked reaction.

Looking down at her surprisingly empty plate, Gina wondered what he had in mind, but told herself that she wasn't going to show the slightest interest.

'Aren't you going to ask me why I need a woman who can cook?' he prodded.

Slowly she raised her eyelids to give him a bored glance from under her long lashes. He grinned again knowingly and pushed his empty plate aside.

'Devastating! I bet you've practised that for years,' he murmured mockingly, and to her annoyance blood rushed to her cheeks. He leaned across the table and brushed a long forefinger down her cheek. 'Now that is real and gives me hope,' he commented. 'Your mother tells me you cook very well.'

'*My* mother?' she exclaimed.

'Yes, I called to see her. She gave me your address and phone number.'

'Why do you need a cook?' she asked. 'You cook very well.'

He inclined his head in mock appreciation of the compli-

18

ment.

'Grudgingly admitted, but at least you admitted it,' he said. 'Have some more coffee while I tell you why.'

Meekly Gina passed her cup. It was the best coffee she had ever tasted.

'Soon after I left the Army I bought a small estate in the Highlands of Scotland. My intention was, and still is, to farm it,' he explained. 'It's good sheep country and I already have a sizeable flock. There are fertile fields and the possibility of rearing some dairy cattle. One day it occurred to me I could share the beauty and peace of the place with others and make a little money on the side. I decided to run an adventure camp for young people of both sexes. I ran into an old friend from my army days who was very interested in the scheme. Last summer we organised our first two camps. They were a great success, but from the point of view of some of the parents of the youngsters attending they had one drawback.'

'What was that?'

'There was no woman on the premises.'

'I understand,' said Gina. 'Couldn't you or your partner get married?'

'He did. Last November, and we thought our problem was solved,' he said drily. 'His wife was very enthusiastic at first. She'd been a social worker in a slum district of Glasgow and she thought up the idea of having groups of poorer youngsters come to the camps. We decided to run one for them this Easter. Now Madge is expecting a child and can't cope. Twenty youngsters are due to arrive next week and we need someone to cook for them.'

'Aren't there any local women willing to help?'

'No. You see the place is situated on the shores of a sea loch which is practically inaccessible from the landward side. There's no electricity. Cooking is done by Calor gas, which I haul in myself from Ullapool. Not many women these days are willing to put up with such conditions. I've interviewed a few and once they've learned that there's no

19

electricity, they've refused. Not many of them have measured up to my standards either,' he added cynically.

'Why don't you get married?' she asked curiously.

His face turned to stone and his eyes went blank.

'What makes you think that having a wife solves anything?' he retorted coldly. 'I tried marriage once. It didn't work.'

Gina raised her eyebrows. He met her glance squarely and smiled.

'I'm not going into details,' he murmured. 'Now when your mother told me that you'd trained in institutional management, and that the doctor had prescribed a complete change of scene for you to recover from the shock of Noll's death, I thought that you might be interested in, and possibly suitable for, the job. That's why I had to see you.'

He paused and glanced round the pretty kitchenette. Then he looked at her, his keen glance taking in the smooth crown of burnished brown hair, the smoothly applied make-up, the close-fitting expensive sweater and the fine white hands holding the coffee cup, and his wide mouth curled jeeringly.

'But now that I've seen you in your nice cosy little nest I realise I'm off-centre,' he said. 'You're the kitten-soft kind of woman who likes comfort, who likes to be adored and waited on, and who likes to be loaded with worldly goods. You're loaded too, aren't you, with money? I suppose that's why Noll wanted to marry you. I daresay you were going into marriage with a handsome annuity behind you, bestowed on you by your old man.'

Gina's fingers gripped the coffee cup. She longed to hurl it at him. His jeers pricked her pride and stabbed painfully at the vulnerable romantic heart she hid beneath her sophistication. It was just possible that Will Fox had hit the mark more closely than she wanted to admit.

'Oliver loved me,' she retorted. 'And I loved him. He would never have wanted to marry me for any other reason.'

Again he raised that infuriating right eyebrow at her.

'You think not?' he queried. 'Naïve, aren't you? Noll was like my mother.'

'And she's one of the most charming people I've ever met,' defended Gina.

'Charming, I grant you, but with an eye to the main chance. Ambitious to the core. You should have seen what she did to my father because he refused to climb any higher in his career. She was the reason why he was always volunteering for jobs where there were no married quarters,' he said, his mouth curving cynically. 'But far be it from me to destroy your illusions about people. Would you come and cook at the spring camp?'

Gina's eyes widened in bewilderment.

'B ... but you've just said I'm not suitable.'

'No, I didn't say that. I said that I didn't think you'd be interested in coming to the back of beyond, now that I've seen you in your setting. But I'm getting pretty desperate now. The boys are due to arrive next Monday. If you decide to come you could travel with me tomorrow, and stay until Madge can cope again. I expect she'd like to have company.'

'I ... I'll think about it,' Gina evaded the issue because it was surprisingly difficult to refuse.

He sighed heavily.

'That means you're not interested. All right, think, and while you're thinking we'll go to Stratford.'

'Oh, no, I can't. I have an appointment in Warwick at two o'clock,' said Gina, glad she had an excuse for retreating.

'An appointment for what?' he demanded.

'A job. With the county education committee's school meals service.'

'Then you can go there after we've been to Stratford,' he replied coolly. 'Do you have a car?'

'Yes, a Triumph Sports.'

'You would,' he remarked drily. 'A present from Daddy,

I've no doubt. We'll go in that. I'm driving a small truck at the moment. Very useful, home on the farm, but not really suitable for driving round the Warwickshire country lanes. Now, you go and make your bed and I'll wash up and then we'll go.'

'I . . . I . . .' stuttered Gina, who was not used to receiving orders.

He stood up and began to gather the dishes together.

'Come on, George, look sharp. It's a lovely spring morning and we're going to miss the best part of the day if you don't get a move on. By the way, who uses the other bedroom?'

'My flat-mate, Bir . . . I mean Lynette.'

'Now there's a name I could like,' he murmured. 'What's she like?'

'Blonde, five feet nine inches. I'm not sure of her other dimensions,' replied Gina with a touch of acidity. She was sure Birdie would like Will Fox. He had the physique and easy confident manner the blonde girl always admired in the opposite sex.

'What does she do for her living?' asked Will casually.

'She's assistant buyer in the women's fashion department of a big department store. Why do you want to know?'

'I'm just trying to find out what she's like and whether she'd object to moving into your room while I use hers tonight. Do you think she would?'

Gina stood there with her mouth agape as the water swished into the sink.

'Mr—I mean Captain Fox, it isn't a case of *her* objecting,' she said at last, 'it's whether I object. This is not a lodging house, nor can it be commandeered as a billet for the Army on the move.'

His grin flashed out and he lifted his shoulders in a careless shrug.

'All right, don't get all upstage at the thought of another woman sharing your bed. I could have offered to share it with you instead, but I thought that would be presuming on

22

our almost close relationship too far. If you don't like the idea I'll sleep on the sofa,' he said.

'You could sleep in a hotel,' sniped Gina, and he gave her a glance of mock-disapproval.

'Now, now, George, that isn't very hospitable of you. Your mother wouldn't approve. I slept in the spare room at your parents' home last night. Very comfortable, too. Go and change your pants for a skirt, and bring a raincoat. There just might be a shower while we're out.'

There was nothing she could have done to prevent it from happening, thought Gina defensively, when she sat in her car half an hour later and watched Will's hands on the steering wheel as he guided the vehicle skilfully through the traffic on the main road going south through the suburb of Solihull. Harking back to the conversation which had taken place at the flat, she realised she hadn't tried very hard. She had gone and changed into the skirt which went with the golden-coloured suit, and she had brought a raincoat, a scarlet one.

The hood of the car was down and the soft spring air lifted the curls at the sides of her face, making them swing. It was, as Will had said, a lovely day. With a strange shock of surprise she noticed that the season had been working its magic in gardens and on the countryside while she had been moping in the flat.

Moping—that was exactly what she had been doing, and she would still be lying there in her bed, her eyes closed against the sunny day, wishing she could die, if this outrageous man had not come this morning and forced her to come with him. No, not forced, he hadn't done that, but it was difficult to describe what he had done. By a series of taunts and suggestions he had made her leave the bed, get dressed, eat and come out with him.

What a misery she must have been during the past week! She had behaved like a spoiled child who had had her favourite playmate taken away from her. Not that she and Oliver had played much together. Theirs had been a serious courtship as suited a young ambitious doctor and the daughter of the managing director of an engineering company.

Yes, Oliver had been very conventional, but his brother was not. Having now met Will it was easy to understand why Oliver had talked so little about him. Understandable too was Mrs Simpson's silence on the subject of her elder son. He just did not fit in the comfortable middle-class community in which Ann Simpson lived and moved. She would always have to be explaining his odd behaviour and comments to her neighbours, who might look askance at someone who preferred to live in a wild inaccessible part of the country and who had tried marriage, but had found it didn't work.

She pondered his terse statement, wondering what matrimonial tangle lay hidden behind it. She imagined Will Fox could be quite difficult to live with and would require a lot of loving. He would also be difficult and demanding to work for. She had said she would think about his suggestion that she should go and cook for his adventure camp more as a way to put him off than anything else, hoping he would leave the flat and go north without her.

But he hadn't left, and it looked as if she was going to be saddled with him for the rest of the day, so any refusal to his offer of a job would have to be made to his face, a task she didn't relish as she was sure he wouldn't accept any excuse she made.

By evening it should be easier to give him a straight flat refusal. She was sure she would be offered a job by the county education committee. Her references were excellent and she had her father's influence behind her. Her mother, too, was well known. Yes, there was really no decision to make. It would be made for her that afternoon at the county offices, and later, safe and sound in the knowledge that she had a job, she would be able to send Will Fox on his way.

Pleased with her thoughts, Gina relaxed in her seat. They had passed through her home town of Henley-in-Arden and were now speeding along the road to Stratford.

The wooded slopes and neatly ploughed fields of the countryside were very familiar to her. Here she had often wandered as a child and, later, as an adolescent searching the woods and hedgerows for the wild flowers, so beloved by Shakespeare, who had wandered here himself, that he had scattered their names liberally throughout his plays. Violets, oxlips, woodbine, musk rose.

'Why do you want to go to Stratford?' she asked Will.

'Although I was born in Leamington, I've never been to Stratford,' he replied. 'I think it's time I went there, because I was christened William Shakespeare.'

Gina exploded into spontaneous laughter. Anyone who looked less like the Bard of Avon than Will Fox was difficult to imagine. It was the first time she had laughed since Oliver had been killed. She didn't know the difference laughter made to her. It drove the serious, slightly supercilious expression from her face and turned her into a natural, fun-loving girl with sparkling eyes, rosy cheeks and glinting white teeth, all of which her companion noticed with approval in his glance.

'Oh no,' she gasped. 'You'll be saying next that Oliver was named after Oliver Cromwell.'

'He was. Ironic, isn't it, that I turned out to be the soldier?' he said.

'He didn't tell me,' she exclaimed.

'He wouldn't,' he commented drily. 'No more than I used to tell anyone my full name for fear of being laughed at. Now I've reached the age when I don't care who laughs at me.'

'Whose idea was it? Your mother's or your father's?'

'I owe my name to my mother. She chose it in a rare moment of romanticism. You see, her maiden name was Hathaway, and that, combined with her christian name of Ann, gave her ideas. She was never able to find a Will Shakespeare to marry, so she called me after him. I think at one time she had a hope that I might live up to the name and become a poet or a playwright. She soon lost that hope

25

when it became very obvious that I was more interested in out-of-door activities than in reading or writing. My father, whose family had always had members in the British Army, retaliated when Noll was born by having him christened after his hero, Oliver Cromwell.'

Gina was laughing again.

'I wonder why he didn't tell me?' she said, when she had her breath back.

'I suspect he went all out to make an impression on you. Probably Mother told him not to tell you. He always tended to follow her advice.'

'He didn't tell me much about you, nor did your mother.'

'For the same reason, I expect. They'd rather you didn't know about me. I've been a great disappointment to them,' he replied cynically.

'Black sheep?' she queried, and saw his crooked grin appear.

'That's as good a description as any,' he said non-committally. 'Do you know Stratford well?'

'Every nook and cranny.'

'I hoped you might, because I want to see all the places —Anne Hathaway's cottage, the Grammar School, Holy Trinity Church, Clopton Bridge, the theatre, the lot.'

'Anne's cottage is at Shottery, and it wasn't really hers. It was called Hewland Farm and belonged to her father. She was just born there.'

'Then we shall go to Shottery too.'

Stratford was busy, but not as crowded as it would be later in the year when the hordes of visitors from overseas would cram into every hotel and guest-house. Gina and Will visited the house on Henley Street where Will Shakespeare's father had lived, then lingered for a while in the old Grammar School with its wooden beams and diamond-paned windows. In the church they stood in silent worship beneath the stone bust of the poet, in the chancel. Soft light, colour-mottled, filtered through the stained glass win-

26

dows, adding to the sense of peace and timelessness.

It was peaceful too at Shottery. The cottage, built of mellow brick and timber and roofed with brown thatch, in that combination of various materials which is a feature of Tudor houses, basked in the April sunlight. Daffodils danced in the garden and birds twittered happily as they flew amongst the many trees and shrubs. Inside, in the kitchen, Gina and Will sat side by side on the narrow wooden settle on which, it is said, Anne Hathaway and Will Shakespeare had done their courting.

'It's more likely that they did their courting in the fields. To quote Shakespeare himself, "Between the acres of the rye,"' said Gina, with a touch of dryness.

'You sound disapproving. What's wrong with courting in the fields in springtime?' asked Will, raising an eyebrow at her.

'Nothing, I suppose,' she said, feeling the blood creep warmly into her cheeks as she encountered the knowing twinkle in his eyes. 'But I suspect he had to marry her because of the consequences of their courting.'

'Poor Will!' he murmured. 'If that was the case, *he* has my sympathy.'

Back in Stratford they paused on the grey Clopton Bridge which spans the river Avon. Once more side by side, they leaned on the old stone wall and watched two white swans glide downstream. Then they drove out of the town to the theatre, finding its bulky twentieth-century structure very different from the Tudor buildings in which they had spent most of their time.

There was no more time to linger. Leaving Stratford, they set out for Warwick. As they drove along country lanes, whose hedges were beginning to burst into leaf, the sky clouded over and rain threatened. In the county town, the walls of the still-inhabited castle loomed grey and formidable over the narrow thoroughfare.

Will left Gina at the front door of the County Council offices, saying he would come back for her in an hour. As he

27

drove away Gina felt suddenly cold and nervous. For the first time since Oliver had been killed she was alone in the world outside her flat. The next step she would make by herself.

Suddenly she realised how much she had enjoyed the time spent with Will in Stratford. She was surprised how much she had known about the place and its famous playwright and how much she had enjoyed sharing that knowledge with Will. He had listened to her attentively, drawing out her knowledge with skilful interested questions, and she had a feeling he had enjoyed the tour as much as she had.

Pulling herself together, she told herself there was no need to be nervous. There would be several people on the interviewing committee whom she would know and she was sure the interview would go easily.

An hour and ten minutes later she emerged from the offices with an expression of bewilderment on her face. Across the road she could see the Triumph parked. Will 'Shakespeare' Fox was lounging behind the steering wheel.

Gina crossed the road quickly and slid into the seat beside him.

'Do you mind if we go back to Birmingham by way of Henley-in-Arden? I must go and see my mother,' she said breathlessly.

His eyes were shrewd as he slanted a glance at her.

'You didn't get the job,' he said.

'No. And I can't think why.'

'For once the magic formula didn't work,' he remarked drily, as he started the car and eased it away from the curb.

'What magic formula?' asked Gina.

'The right surname, the right contacts as well as the right qualifications,' he replied, with a touch of sarcasm. 'I presume you have all those for this area, and yet they chose an experienced stranger.'

'Yes, they did. But how do you know?'

'Fortunately it happens all the time, otherwise the taxpayer might have good reason to complain,' he remarked drily. Then, more gently, as he noticed the expression of distress on her face, 'The job as cook for the spring camp is still open.'

Gina looked out at the fields and woods, blurred now as the rain became more than a threat.

'I'm still thinking about it,' she said lamely.

'But it would have been much easier if the decision had been made for you by the offer of that job with the county,' he jibed. 'All right, think away.'

They reached Green Willows, her parents' house, just as the rain began to fall heavily. Gina left the car to run into the house, leaving Will to adjust the hood to keep the seats of the car dry.

Her mother came to the door in answer to her ringing and regarded her with surprised brown eyes.

'Gina, how lovely! Oh, how much better you look,' she exclaimed. She glanced past her daughter at the car. 'Who's with you?'

'Will Fox,' said Gina shortly, stepping into the hallway and removing her raincoat.

'He did call you, then. I rather hoped he would. Such a pleasant man. We had a very jolly evening with him. Your father was most impressed by him.'

'Mother,' said Gina, interrupting the flow of her mother's words which, she knew from experience, would go on for ever if no one interrupted, 'I've just come from an interview for that job with the county education committee. I didn't get it.'

Dilys Marriott was a slightly built, dark-haired Welsh woman. She wore a perpetually surprised expression on her fine-boned face. This expression did not alter as she turned to look at Gina and it was difficult to guess whether she knew anything about the interview or not.

'Didn't you, dear?' she said smoothly. 'Well, don't be too disappointed. It wouldn't have been much of a change for you. You'd have still been here in Warwickshire, near all

29

the places you used to visit with Oliver.'

Will came in, closed the front door and Mrs Marriott went forward to meet him.

'How nice to see you again, so soon,' she said warmly. 'Let me take your raincoat. My goodness, you did get wet! It started off such a nice day. We're just going to have afternoon tea in the lounge. Come and join us. Then you'll both stay to dinner, of course. Your father will want to see you, Gina dear.'

They followed her across the thick pile carpet and down two shallow steps into the big lounge which was a long, low-ceilinged room with wide windows at each end looking out on to well-tended gardens.

To Gina's surprise and secret horror there were already several women in the lounge, all of them engaged in different forms of needlework. With a cold feeling of dismay she stopped short and stared at them. They stopped talking and stared at her, and then beyond her at Will.

'We're sewing for the church bazaar,' explained Mrs Marriott.

'Then we'll go into the library,' said Gina desperately, in full retreat, wanting to escape from that curious sympathetic battery of eyes.

'No, of course not,' said her mother firmly. 'They'll all be so pleased to see you and quite delighted to have Will to tea with them. Come along now and I'll introduce you, Will.'

While Gina stood uncertainly, Dilys took Will by the arm and led him forward. He didn't seem at all ill at ease, although Gina suspected that inside he was laughing to himself. Reluctantly, her face burning, she followed in their wake.

'Nice to see you, Gina,' boomed a voice on her left. 'Come and sit beside me and tell me what you've been doing with yourself, girl.'

She glanced sideways and recognised, with relief, the vicar's sister, who had once been a teacher of gymnastics at the local grammar school. She sat down beside her and was immediately swamped with local news because the vicar's sister didn't really want to hear about Gina Marriott, but required merely a receptive ear for her gossip.

At five o'clock the women were seen off by Dilys, who lingered in the hall to speak to each one in turn. In the lounge Gina took a biscuit from one of the plates and curled up on the big chesterfield. She glanced at the broad back of the man who was standing in the window embrasure looking out at the rain.

'Your behaviour was exemplary,' she said. 'How did you do it and not laugh?'

He swung round and came slowly towards her. Hands in his pockets he stood over her. His mouth was grim and his eyes were like blue flints. Gina shivered a little.

'If mine was exemplary, yours was disgraceful,' he said softly. 'You deserve to be spanked, you spoilt little cat.'

He didn't tell her why she deserved to be spanked because her mother came back into the room. Gina thought she had never been spoken to by anyone like that before, nor had she ever been spanked. And what was more, she couldn't think why he thought she deserved such treatment. As far as she knew she'd done nothing wrong. She'd sat beside Miss Berry and had listened to her ramblings, knowing she was safe there and wouldn't have to face up to the expressions of sympathy which would have been her lot if she had spoken to any of the other women.

In the half-coma produced by the effort of pretending to listen to Miss Berry she had been vaguely aware of Will handing round tea for her mother, passing plates of sandwiches and cakes and generally making himself useful as well as pleasant, much to her surprise. She had thought, judging him by his behaviour in the flat that morning, that he would have sat apart, silently ridiculing the bazaar ladies' type of conversation, as Oliver would have done. But, instead of doing that, he had joined in.

Even now he was helping her mother to remove the remains of the tea party, carrying out a laden tray and coming back for another. As he passed by the end of the chesterfield he glanced at her and ordered brusquely,

'Come on, George, look alive. There's plenty to do. Your mother isn't getting any younger, you know. In fact she's just gone upstairs to have a rest before dinner.'

She blinked up at him.

'But Mummy hardly ever rests.'

'Well, she's resting now. Her legs are aching, she says. You and I are going to rinse the crockery and put it in the dishwasher and put away the food, and then you're going to cook the dinner, just to show me whether you're any good at it or not,' he announced calmly.

'But Mrs Brooks always . . .'

'Mrs Brooks has the 'flu, and isn't here today. Nor has she been here all week. And it's time you stopped depending on the older generation to do your work for you. Now, are you going to move voluntarily, or am I going to make you?' he threatened, coming to stand over her again.

Gina moved. Head held high, she went through to the kitchen and started on the dishes. He came to help her and they worked in silence. Secretly worried about her mother, Gina worked quickly and efficiently, conscious all the time of waves of disapproval being relayed from Will to herself. She kept telling herself that she didn't care whether he approved of her behaviour or not and that he had no right to be so critical of her, but she could not help wondering whether he was right, and she was spoilt.

As soon as the dishwasher was going and the food had been put away, she excused herself, saying she was going to see her mother to ask what was for dinner. Glancing at Will in her most supercilious manner, she suggested that he went to sit in the library or the lounge and to make himself at home until her father returned.

Upstairs her parents' bedroom was as it had always been, a pleasant comfortable haven; a place to which she had scurried in the night as a child disturbed by nightmares, to climb into the big bed beside her mother, knowing that she would be safe there.

Dilys was lying on the bed idly turning the pages of a magazine.

'Mummy, are your legs really aching?' asked Gina, approaching the bed.

Dilys glanced at her, an amused twinkle in her eyes.

'Yes, they really are. So nice of you to offer to clear up after the tea party and to say you'd cook the dinner. Poor Mrs Brooks isn't at all well. The 'flu left her with bronchitis.'

Gina opened her mouth to say that she hadn't offered to clear up or to make the dinner, then closed it again as she realised the offer had been made on her behalf by that infuriating, interfering man downstairs.

Then remembering his criticism of her, she sat down on the side of the bed, fiddling with the gold charm bracelet which had been a twenty-first birthday present to her from Oliver.

'Mummy, would you say I'm spoilt?' she asked suddenly.

'A little, yes. But it's natural for you to be. You're our only daughter and perhaps your father and I have been easier with you than with the boys and have given you most of the things you've asked for. You've been easy to spoil because you've always been so pretty and good-natured. Why do you ask?'

'Something which happened today made me wonder if I am.'

'Not getting the job?' Dilys's eyes were shrewd.

'Yes, but not only that. You see, when Will Fox made me go out with him, I realised for the first time since Oliver was killed how awful and miserable I'd been and how badly I've been treating everyone. You, and Daddy, and Birdie and Mrs Simpson, you must have all been terribly fed up with me.'

'No, dear, not fed up. None of us could ever be that. But

we have been very concerned about you. I suppose I showed my concern to Will when he called to see us yesterday. I thought it was nice of him to call. He'd been to see his mother to give her his sympathy on the death of Oliver and to explain why he wasn't able to arrive in time for the funeral. Apparently the road where he lives was made impassable by the spring rains. It must be a very remote place. He did tell me its name, but I can never remember those Scottish names.'

'It's somewhere in the Highlands,' muttered Gina.

'That's right, and he's allowing it to be used by some organisation for underprivileged youths over the Easter holidays. Very good of him, I thought. Anyway, he asked for your address and said he'd call on you and try to persuade you to go for a drive somewhere. I'm glad he succeeded. You look so much better. Your cheeks are quite pink and your eyes are brighter.'

Persuasion! So that was William Fox's name for the tactics he'd used that morning, thought Gina, suddenly indignant again.

'You like him better than you liked Oliver,' she accused her mother.

Dilys sighed and closed her eyes. Then, opening them, she looked rather pityingly at her only daughter, the child on whom she had lavished so much of her love. She knew that Gina was innately shy and affectionate, yet she also knew that the young woman could be very stubborn at times. The stubbornness had shown itself particularly over the matter of her marriage to the punctilious, ambitious Oliver.

'I didn't dislike Oliver,' she explained slowly. 'I just thought you should have waited longer before deciding to marry. After all, Gina, he was the only young man you'd ever known. You can't say that they've been queueing up to take you out over the years, can you?'

That was true. Although attractive to look at, Gina had not had any boy-friends because she was shy, and she hid

34

that shyness under a façade of sophistication which had tended to frighten young men away. Only Oliver had persisted in getting to know her and, because of that persistence on his part, she had believed him to be in love with her and had consequently fallen in love with him.

'Oliver and I were ideally suited to each other,' she defended shakily, tears springing to her eyes as they often did since Oliver had died. 'We liked the same things. We never quarrelled. Our marriage would have been perfect.'

'No marriage is ever that,' murmured Dilys. 'Not at the start, at any rate. It might grow to perfection over the years as the partners learn what love is all about.' Then seeing that Gina was very upset, she patted her hand comfortingly. 'I just felt that sometimes Oliver's approach to you was rather calculated and that your relationship seemed cut and dried. Arid, almost. No surprises, no excitement. There was nothing unpredictable about Oliver. You would always have known where you were with him, which might have led to dullness later. I suppose I'm an old-fashioned romantic at heart, but I used to feel that you weren't in love with each other, at least not in the way David and I were, and still are. There, we won't talk about it any more because I can see it's upsetting you. Will you stay the night? Michael will be home from Oxford for the week-end. He's bringing a college friend with him. Captain Fox is welcome to stay the night with us again.'

'No, thank you. We won't stay,' said Gina hurriedly. 'I promised Birdie that I'd help her with a party she's giving. I'll come down again tomorrow. I'll have to start looking for another job.'

'Have you anything in mind?'

'No. I was so sure I'd get the job with the county. Of course I could take the job that Will Fox has offered me.'

'What is that?'

'He needs a cook for the spring camp. His partner's wife is expecting her first baby soon and can't manage very well. I've a feeling he doesn't expect me to take it. He thinks I'm

CHAPTER TWO

'BUT you're not a bit like Oliver. You can't be his brother.' Birdie's exclamation, when Gina introduced Will to her at the flat, was an echo of Dilys' remark.

He had accompanied Gina to the door of the flat, much to her surprise because she had thought he would have left her outside the building. He had come with her, he said, because he had left his briefcase in the flat.

'I can assure you I'm his brother. Same parents, just a different combination of genes,' said Will jovially, his glance roving appreciatively over Birdie, tall and Junoesque in a long clinging black evening gown with a deep plunge neckline which left little to the imagination. 'Where have you been all my life?' he added provocatively.

Birdie's wide knowledgeable blue eyes twinkled back at him.

'Right here, Will, waiting for you to turn up. I hope you'll stay for the party. Come into the kitchen and help me sort out the drinks while Gina goes and changes. It's as good a way as any I know of getting to know one another better.'

'Lead the way, Birdie. I'd love to know *you* better,' he replied with a grin, and Birdie chuckled delightedly as she tucked a long white arm through one of his.

'Oh, William, you're just the boost this girl's morale was needing.'

They went off to the kitchenette together apparently having forgotten Gina, who went on to her own room. The bed was still unmade and Blue was curled up on the corner of the eiderdown which trailed on the floor. He greeted her excitedly when she flopped down on to the bed.

'Oh, Blue,' she whispered to the furry, purring animal, 'what am I going to do? I think Will Fox has forgotten that he offered me a job.'

She had hoped to bring up the subject of the job as cook at the spring camp during the drive back to Birmingham, but she had found it difficult to communicate with her companion, who had been silent and reserved, concentrating on driving in the pouring rain.

His withdrawn manner came as a surprise because during dinner with her parents, her youngest brother Michael and his college friend, Will had been pleasant and talkative.

But in the darkness of the little car she had felt once again that he disapproved of her, even disliked her. His dislike had arisen, she guessed, from his observance of her behaviour at the tea-party. He had seen her at her worst, he thought, and now he wanted nothing more to do with her. She longed to tell him that she hadn't behaved badly deliberately, that she had only shrunk from the social occasion, in the same way she was shrinking from Birdie's party now, because she didn't want anyone to pity her. But she had found it completely impossible to communicate with him when he had ignored her.

And now he and Birdie had met the chances of approaching him were fading fast. They were obviously attracted to one another on sight. 'No sooner looked than loved.' Was that how it would be with them?

Impatient with her thoughts, she pushed Blue to the floor and stood up. If she didn't go to the party she wouldn't be able to rest because of the noise. Birdie's parties were always very gay and very noisy, which was why she and Oliver had always avoided them. Also, she had to make sure Will Fox did not monopolise Birdie too much. Robin Carlton, who had been taking Birdie out for some months, would be coming, and Gina was convinced he was in love with Birdie.

Going to the wardrobe, she selected one of the evening dresses she had bought for her trousseau. It was made of fine wool and was patterned in deep greens and blues. A pleat from the seam just under the high bustline gave it a mediaeval effect. It had a simple low curved neckline and full three-quarter-length sleeves. With her hair let down from its chignon and drawn back from her face to hang in rippling curls down her back, Gina looked elegant yet youthful as she entered the living room.

She did not realise that the dress emphasised her softness, giving her a pampered look in the eyes of Will Fox, who surveyed her with a slight sneer curving his mouth. He was lounging on the settee with Birdie. One of his arms rested on the back of the seat behind his hostess and his hand touched the top of Birdie's bare arm. Noting the intimacy with which he was already treating her friend, Gina determined to be as pleasant and as kind to Robin when he came.

When Robin did arrive he looked rather dumbfounded by the sight of Birdie on such good terms with the lively Will, and immediately Gina's determination increased. For the first time in her life she exerted herself to hold a man's attention. Robin responded rather half-heartedly, but as the party became noisier and noisier, he seemed to grow more and more disheartened as Birdie ignored him, finding in Will someone who could cap her own humorous remarks with outrageous witticisms which set everyone roaring with laughter.

Then at one point someone asked Will where he was staying for the night in Birmingham. He considered the question with apparent seriousness and looking straight at Gina said,

'I'm staying here. As a matter of fact I'm hoping to move into Birdie's room.'

No one took his remark seriously except Gina herself and Robin, who muttered,

'I can't stand any more of this,' and left the room.

Hurrying after him, Gina tried to persuade him to stay, but he was too angry to listen and left the flat banging the door behind him.

If Birdie noticed his absence she said nothing, and the

party went on, although, without Robin, Gina lost interest and eventually retired to her bedroom.

There she made the bed and began to undress. What a day it had been! She felt as if a whirlwind had entered her life when Will Fox had entered her room. Nothing had been the same since then. All her preconceptions about people had been upset. He had made her start questioning about herself, about Oliver and now about Birdie.

She had known Birdie since her days at the Grammar School. They had spent holidays together. Yet what did she really know about her? She had always thought her kindly if a little scatterbrained. But after this evening she was beginning to wonder about Birdie's morals.

Realising the direction her thoughts were taking, Gina found her face burning. Was Will Fox really going to stay the night in the flat? There was only one way to find out. She must go and see if he had left with the others. The noise from the living room had died down now although she could still hear the record player and, above it, people calling out good night, followed by the sound of the flat door closing.

Opening the door of her room a crack, she listened. All was quiet except for the sound of soft music. Gina stepped out into the passage and went along to the living room. She walked in and stopped dead. On the settee were two people entwined in a close embrace. Birdie and the ex-Army Captain, of course.

Her heart beating fast, Gina whirled and retreated along the passage to her room. Closing the door, she leaned against it, trying to calm her agitation. What could she do? Nothing, really. Birdie and Will were adults and what they did together was none of her business. Why, then, did she have this strange sense of disappointment? She had thought better of Birdie. As for Will Fox—well, there wasn't anything she would put past him.

The rest of the night seemed interminable. She couldn't sleep. Every time she turned on the bedside lamp and stretched out her hand to the bottle of sleeping pills prescribed by the doctor there flashed across her memory the image of Will's mouth twisted into a sneer and she heard his voice, almost as if he were there in the room with her, asking her if they were the drug she used to forget reality. Immediately her hand withdrew from the container, she switched out the light and flung over on her other side to woo sleep once more.

The trouble was her imagination was too vivid. She kept thinking of Birdie and Will as she had last seen them kissing on the settee in the living room. It was strange that it should bother her. Over the past few months Robin Carlton had stayed late with Birdie in the living room and Gina hadn't given it a thought.

Ruefully she had to admit it was because Will Fox had been there tonight. He was unpredictable. She couldn't be sure what he was really like. She had changed her mind about him several times already.

Dawn crept stealthily into the room, filling it with pearl grey light. Gina gave up trying to sleep and decided to go into the kitchen to make herself a cup of tea. It was only six-thirty. That meant the day was going to be long, a wasteland without Oliver. Perhaps she would go home and spend the day with her parents, and maybe tomorrow she would visit her eldest brother Luke and his wife and their new baby. Anything to fill in the empty hours.

To her surprise the living room was tidy, all the debris of the party having been swept away as if by a clean broom. Cushions had been plumped and ash trays had been emptied. Everything had a shining look. The settee did not look as if anyone had slept on it, and immediately Gina's heart plummeted. Where was Will Fox?

She went to the kitchen, and this time her heart leapt up. Someone was there before her, someone who was whistling a familiar tune, a folk song she had once heard with a slyly seductive lyric, something to do with lifting a woman's petticoat to buckle her shoe.

'Good morning, George.'

Will was pouring boiling water into the tea-pot. He was clean-shaven and was wearing a different shirt. He was alert and bright-eyed and, apart from a few tell-tale lines under his eyes, she would have thought he had slept a full eight hours during the night. He made her feel more jaded than ever and she resented him.

'Good morning,' she replied coldly. 'So you did stay the night after all.'

'I did. But it's time I was on my way north. I've dallied in the lush pastures of the enervating south long enough. Have you finished thinking yet?'

'About what?' she countered.

'My suggestion that you should come north with me.'

'After last night I'd have thought you'd have asked Birdie to go with you,' she said, still cold.

'Miaow,' he retorted with a grin. Then, sobering, he added, 'I didn't mention it to her. She's a great girl, lots of fun to be with. She and I...' he paused and gave her an enigmatic glance. 'Do you think she'd come if I asked her?' he queried with a touch of earnestness which was oddly disarming, giving her the impression that for once he was uncertain and needed encouragement.

But Gina was not disposed to encourage him in that direction. Birdie must not be given the chance to go north with him and cook at his adventure camp. There was Robin Carlton to be considered. Besides, Birdie couldn't cook!

'No. I don't think she would,' she replied firmly. 'You see, she likes her work here and she's in line for promotion soon. Actually I had finished thinking and I'd come to the conclusion that perhaps I could help you out, on a purely voluntary basis, until your partner's wife is able to tackle the work again. Would that be of any use to you?' she asked, in the manner of someone conferring a great favour.

He was busy pouring tea into three cups, and he did not answer at once. When he'd finished pouring he glanced at her thoughtfully.

'You're not exactly the sort of person I had in mind,' he said slowly, 'but I'm inclined to accept your magnanimous offer because I've always worked on the theory that one volunteer is better than several pressed men. Thanks, George, I'll be glad of your help. And now I must take this cup of tea to Birdie. I think I owe it to her.'

He didn't say why he owed the cup of tea to Birdie, but left the kitchen before Gina could remonstrate. She followed him into the passage just in time to see him go into Birdie's room and close the door behind him. A few seconds later she heard them laughing together. She had the most uncomfortable feeling that the joke they were sharing was on her. Hands clenched by her sides, she returned to the kitchen to drink her tea and give Blue his morning milk.

As she set the saucer on the floor for the kitten, the enormity of her recent impulsive decision to go north with Will Fox that day and stay in his wilderness to cook for twenty youths became more apparent. Whatever had she been thinking of? What had goaded her into offering to help him for nothing? She must be out of her mind. Going over the conversation which had led up to her making her offer she realised, with a sense of astonishment at her own peculiar behaviour, that she had offered merely because she hadn't wanted him to ask Birdie.

The telephone shrilled suddenly in the living room. Almost tripping over her dressing gown, she rushed to it to make sure she answered it before Will did. It would never do for him to answer it at this time of the morning.

Robin answered her breathless greeting. He wanted to speak to Birdie. Gina told him to hang on and, glad to see that Will had gone back to the kitchen, she went into her friend's room.

Birdie, looking curiously angelic in a white crocheted bed-jacket with full sleeves, was sitting up in bed. She greeted Gina with a smile and raised her tea cup.

'Look what William the Conqueror brought me,' she said.

'The Conqueror? Why do you call him that?' exclaimed Gina.

'Oh, he just strikes me as being the sort of man who sees and conquers,' replied Birdie, airily.

'Birdie, did you ... I mean ... did he ... Where did he sleep last night?' stammered Gina.

Birdie's eyes widened.

'On the settee in the living room, I suppose. That's where he said he'd sleep.' Then as understanding dawned on her she exclaimed, 'You didn't really believe him when he said he was going to move in with me? Oh, honestly, Gina, how could you?'

'Quite easily. The last I saw of you both you were in a very convincing clinch, and he hardly left your side all evening. In fact poor Robin was—oh, heavens, I forgot! Robin is on the phone. He wants to speak to you urgently.'

'Why didn't you tell me? Here, for goodness' sake take this cup and saucer. Oh, it worked, it worked! It must have worked. Oh, darling William the Conqueror, however can I thank you enough?' sang Birdie as she got out of bed and sped from the room, leaving a completely bewildered Gina holding the cup and saucer.

Pulling herself together, Gina went along to the kitchen again where Will was eating his breakfast and reading the Saturday morning newspaper.

'Your tea is going cold. Better pour some more,' he said practically. 'And eat well. I don't stop for snacks when I'm driving.'

'But I don't think I can be ready to leave today,' said Gina.

'Why? What is there to do except pack a few clothes and your toothbrush?' he asked. 'Take jeans and shirts and loads of sweaters, if you have any. And warm pyjamas. We have plenty of draughts up north. You won't need an evening dress, much as I liked the one you wore last night. There aren't any bright lights where I live.'

44

'Captain Fox——' she began, but he raised his voice above hers and continued to issue orders.

'Let's see, it's now seven-fifteen. We should be able to leave at nine. I'll make some sandwiches. Have you a thermos flask? Good. We can take coffee too. I can eat while I'm driving with you there to hand me the food. That means we can keep going and should reach Loch Lomond this evening. We can stay the night there with a relative of mine. Now, as soon as Birdie stops talking to Robin . . .'

'How do you know she's talking to him?' interrupted Gina, and he gave her an irritated, slightly scornful glance.

'Do you think she'd leave her bed in such a hurry to speak to anyone else?' he countered. 'As I was saying, as soon as she gets off the phone you telephone your parents and tell them where you're going. Then pack your bags while I bring the truck round. Anything else you have to do?'

Gina felt panic rising within her. Wildly she looked for reasons to delay their departure.

'Yes, of course there is, and I'd just like to make it clear here and now that I'm not a subordinate soldier whom you have to brief before sending him on a mission,' she said coldly. 'I know perfectly well what I have to do before I can leave here. I need more time. I can't give up half a flat just like that.' She snapped her fingers. 'Someone will have to take over my share of it. And what about Blue, my kitten?'

'What about Blue?' he drawled, rather menacingly, she thought.

'I can't desert him. Oliver gave him to me.'

'Won't Birdie look after him for you until you come back?'

'I don't think he'd stay with her or anyone else,' she replied, seeing a loophole through which she might escape.

'No cats,' he returned tersely.

'No cat, no me,' she retorted grandly.

For a moment there was deadlock as they stared at each

45

other. Then with a careless shrug of his shoulders Will said,

'All right, bring him. But don't blame me if he gets lost, or drowned, or is shot. Well, that's the cat sorted out. I don't think you'll have any serious trouble in getting rid of your share of the flat. Young Robin will be moving in soon.'

'Young Robin,' she repeated. 'You talk as if you were old enough to be his uncle.'

'That's how I feel, sometimes—like an uncle, giving the younger generation the benefit of my hard-won experience of life,' he remarked, and bitterness carved lines beside his expressive mouth.

'But not Birdie's uncle,' observed Gina with pseudo-sweetness. 'Uncles don't usually embrace their nieces passionately.'

His quick grin was shameless.

'I thought I heard you come into the living room. You can blame that little incident on my proximity all evening to a beautiful blonde. She went to my head and I got carried away by the part I was playing,' he replied blandly, rising to his feet. 'If you've finished eating I'll clear away while you phone your parents. If you have any problems in explaining to them, let me talk to them.'

She had no problems. Her father seemed delighted by the idea and told her not to worry about the flat or any other business because he would look after that for her.

'It'll do you good to get away. Nothing like a change to help you forget,' he said.

She was about to say that she would never forget Oliver and didn't want to forget him when she realised that she had not thought of him since yesterday. She had been too busy. Oliver hadn't even been the cause of her sleepless night. His brother had taken over in that respect.

Her mother was also enthusiastic about her decision to go north.

'Three or four weeks should do the trick,' she said comfortingly, 'and then you'll be ready to come back and face up to normal life again. Write to me as soon as you get there and let me know what it's like.'

Her telephoning done, Gina went in to see Birdie again to tell her she was leaving that day. She found her friend in an ecstatic mood, trying to decide what to wear.

'Oh. Gina, I'm so happy! Robin has asked me to marry him. He said he couldn't wait until he got here. See what a little competition does for a man, even if it was only pretence.'

'You mean you and Will behaved as you did last night deliberately in order to make Robin jealous?'

'Yes. As soon as I met Will I guessed he would be the sort of person who wouldn't mind playing up to my lead. He did it very well, don't you think?' laughed Birdie.

'Too well. I was the only spectator for the big love scene.' remarked Gina drily. 'Robin had left long before that.'

'Oh. that,' said Birdie, and to Gina's astonishment she blushed rosily. 'I suppose it wasn't really necessary, but somehow it happened so naturally, and it was nice.' The expression on Birdie's face changed to one of grave seriousness. 'Gina, are you sure about going to this place where Will lives? It might be a bit rough, not like living here, you know.'

'I know. I'm going to prove to him that I'm not spoilt and pampered, and that I can work as hard as anyone. At the same time I'll be helping his partner's wife. She'll probably be glad of the company of another woman. It isn't a permanent job. I volunteered to do it and can leave when I'm ready. I'll probably be back here in time to be your bridesmaid.'

'I hope so. I was going to ask you, but I didn't like to because it isn't long since you were going to be the bride and I was going to be the bridesmaid,' said Birdie. 'I wish it had all turned out differently for you, Gina, and I hope you won't let losing Oliver stop you falling in love with someone else.'

'I'll try not to, but at the moment I feel as if I'll never

47

fall in love again,' sighed Gina, her eyes filling with tears. 'It's so painful when you lose the one you love.'

The journey to the wilds of Scotland was worse than a nightmare to Gina. Accustomed to travelling in comfort, she found the cab of the small truck which Will owned noisy and draughty. The seat was hard making it difficult for her to relax. Her companion's determination to reach Loch Lomond that day meant that he drove at a steady fast pace once they were on the northbound motorway. He did not bother to entertain her with small talk and there was no radio.

Lunch was taken somewhere between Manchester and Lancaster as they roared along at a steady seventy miles per hour. It was impossible at that speed to pour scalding hot coffee into a plastic cup without spilling it on to her light beige pants. It was almost impossible to drink the stuff because every time she raised her cup to her lips the truck lurched quite unnecessarily, she thought, and she and the cup failed to make contact.

The simple needs of nature seemed not to affect the Army at all, and then, when Will did condescend to stop, he did so on a windy, rainswept stretch of road amongst the bleak fells of Westmorland. She had to climb over a dry stone wall, only to land in a swamp the other side in which she dropped Blue so that the Persian complained bitterly.

When she finally fought her way back across the road to the truck and its waiting whistling driver, she had to brave his derisive glance which took in her dishevelled hair, coffee-stained, rain-soaked pants and muddy, bedraggled animal.

'You might as well get used to living close to nature,' he mocked, 'because where we're going there's nothing else but moors and mountains and water.'

As they forged forward through the mist-laden fells Gina began to feel the effects of her sleepless night. She tried to doze, but there was nothing for her to rest her head against. It kept nodding forward. She would feel as if she were falling and she would jerk it up again and peer blearily out of the rain-spotted windscreen, then doze off again. The jerking happened several times, making her feel thoroughly wretched.

She wished she was at home curled up on the chesterfield at Green Willows, watching the Saturday afternoon sports programme on the television, looking forward to afternoon tea as served by her mother, or alternatively, shopping in Birmingham and then going on to the cinema or to the repertory theatre to see a good play.

'You can try my shoulder, if you like.' Will's voice came as a shock, breaking through the cloud of sleepiness which hovered around her. She glanced at the shoulder in question. It looked sturdy and stable. Having made his offer he seemed unconcerned as to whether she tried it or not. Shifting a little closer to him, she leaned her head against the upper part of his arm, her eyelids drooped, and in no time she was asleep.

The sound of voices roused Gina. Opening her eyes, she blinked in a puzzled way, wondering where she was. Beneath her cheek the tweed of Will's jacket was rough, yet comforting, and she was loath to sit up.

Eventually she became aware that they had stopped for petrol and that the boy attending to the pump was staring through the window at her in an interested way, a cheeky knowing smile curving his mouth. He had a long-jawed freckled face and, from beneath his cap, tufts of sandy hair stuck out. Something about his face spelt Scottish to her.

'Where are we?' she muttered, sitting up and trying to tidy her hair with her hands. Leaning down, she picked up her handbag and brought out her compact. Snapping it open, she glanced at her face and hair, and nearly passed out with shock. One of her cheeks, the one which had been resting against the hospitable Harris tweed, was red and the other was quite pale. Her hair was straggling down from its chignon and her eyes looked slightly bloodshot. Her lipstick was non-existent! She looked literally as if she had been

49

pulled through a hedge backwards. No wonder the boy was grinning!

'Lockerbie,' answered Will briefly, flexing his shoulder and arm as if they were stiff from having supported her.

'In Scotland?'

'Yes.'

He turned away to pay the boy. Since they had stopped perhaps there was a chance that he would let her go to the women's room to clean up, if the petrol station had such a place. If not, perhaps they could go for a cup of tea at a café in the town. Hurriedly she asked him as he stuffed his wallet back into his inside pocket. As if he hadn't heard her he reached out to turn on the ignition, and the engine roared into life. Before releasing the brakes he glanced at her critically.

'You have a comb, haven't you?' he asked, and she nodded. 'Well, use it,' he barked. 'And let's get this straight before we go any further. Where you're going no one is going to worry if you don't look like the latest model out of a women's magazine. Least of all shall I worry. Cleanliness and neatness is all that is required. You're coming to work, not to stand around looking decorative.'

The truck lurched forward and turned out into the road. Gina had a confused impression of a narrow rain-washed street lined with plain-fronted shops and houses, all huddled together as if for comfort, and then they were on a fairly new wide road, still heading north.

On either side of the road green fields, looking dank and desolate under a grey sky, stretched away to gently curving hills. Beyond the hills she could just see the bulk of higher hills, also grey like the sky. Here and there a row of dark pines marched up a hillside and in the corners of fields, bare deciduous trees spread forlorn, dripping branches.

With an exaggerated sigh for the benefit of her companion, Gina peered once more at her reflection and struggled to comb her hair. It wasn't easy to do with one hand, so in the end she unpinned the chignon and tied the released

50

long tresses with a chiffon scarf she had brought. Using a freshening pad, she cleaned off her old make-up and didn't apply any more. Then she sat back and looked out of the window.

They seemed to be quite high up now and the rain was more like mist swirling around them. Water sprayed up from the wheels of traffic passing in the opposite direction, flinging mud at the windscreen of the truck.

Whatever happened to springtime? thought Gina, as she looked out at the bleak scene. The hills had crowded closely about the road now and she could see water cascading down the dark glistening rock. She thought of the daffodils nodding their heads in the garden of the cottage at Shottery the previous day and of the fresh tufts of green sprinkling the hawthorn hedges in Warwickshire. Here there were no hedges and no daffodils, only the dark primeval walls running across the open land and a few weirdly-shaped pine trees. And the villages through which they passed had none of the warmth of mellow brick or golden stone, but were pale grey and secretive-looking.

From the rear of the truck came the plaintive cry of the cat, but Gina knew better than to ask the uncommunicative driver of the vehicle to stop. Nor did she wish to get out of the truck in this weather to duck behind a stone wall again only to return to some derisive remark. So she sat silent, once again wondering what had possessed her to go north with him.

The rest of the journey was miserable in the extreme as she grew more and more cramped and more and more hungry. Hamilton was a mass of factory chimneys and endless dark streets, then they were on the outskirts of Glasgow, then in the city itself beside a muddy turbulent river, crossing a bridge amidst slow-crawling traffic which made her companion curse vividly and fluently with little concern for her gently-reared ears.

Once over the bridge they turned left along a main thoroughfare where lights were glittering and the Saturday

51

afternoon shoppers were still crowding the pavements. Then back to the river they went. It was charcoal grey now, under low tumbled clouds.

Gradually the city was left behind. Ahead Gina could see the dim outline of mountains beyond a wider stretch of water. Lights flashed, sometimes red and sometimes white. Something vague and shadowy, ablaze with light, floated on the water and she realised it was a ship moving down the estuary.

Soon they were passing through another town past an old castle, turning right up a hill into the darkness of the countryside again. Lights once more ahead and they were in the town of Alexandria. There were people queueing up for a cinema, pubs opening their doors, a fish and chip shop where she could see people leaning on the counter waiting to be served. She could almost smell the fish and chips and her stomach gurgled suddenly, noisily.

'Not far now,' murmured Will comfortingly, the first time he had spoken since he had sworn on the bridge. She couldn't see him properly now. He was only a bulky shape in the dim light; a profile occasionally illuminated by the lights of a passing car.

How did he do it? she wondered. How did he keep up the steady pace without stopping or flagging? It must be the Army training, this ability to go on until the destination was reached. He would be terrible to work for, making the same demands on her that he made on himself, and expecting her to respond. Whatever had possessed her to volunteer to come with him?

One more town to go, smaller this time, and then the countryside again and to the right a wide expanse of nothing. No, not nothing. She could just make out the faint gleam of water. It must be a lake. Careful, Gina, they call them *lochs* in this part of the world. Could it be Loch Lomond at last? she asked her companion. His answer was brief. It was.

They turned off the road on to another narrower one. A

house glowing with light loomed out of the darkness. It was long and low.

They stopped before a flight of shallow steps leading to a black-painted door. The engine of the truck was stopped. The silence was blessed to Gina's ears, but it was split almost immediately by the harsh impertinent blare of the truck's horn as Will announced their arrival to whoever was in the house.

The black door swung open. Light poured out showing up the slanting silvery rain. Two figures appeared, slim and adolescent, both with fluffy hair, both in pants. It was difficult to tell whether they were boys or girls or one of each. One of them began to jump up and down with excitement, and when Will opened the door of the vehicle, the jumping figure turned and scampered back into the house. Gina could hear a shrill voice yelling.

'Mum, it's Will! He's come after all!'

The other figure skipped forward, not seeming to mind the rain. Will jumped down, picked whoever it was up in his arms and whirled it round. There were squeals of delight.

Gina supposed she had better get out and see to her poor neglected kitten. She opened the door at her side and, moving rather stiffly, stepped down, splosh into a puddle.

The voice she could hear speaking to Will was that of a girl, and as she walked carefully round the back of the vehicle, she could see Will walking with the girl towards the house. As he put a foot on the lowest step he turned and called out,

'Come on, George, don't be shy.'

It seemed to Gina that he phrased everything he said to her deliberately so as to annoy her.

'I'm coming,' she snapped back. 'But I'd like to let Blue out first, if you don't mind.'

Saying something rude, which was almost inaudible but not quite, about the cat, Will strode back to the truck, opened the canvas cover which protected the back of it, and reached in for Blue. The kitten wailed miserably as it felt the rain on its fur, struggled a little and jumped from Will's hands. It ran away into the wet darkness.

'Oh, Blue!' wailed Gina, who was feeling damp, stiff and miserable herself and had no desire to go searching an unknown garden for her pet.

'Don't worry. I'll find him,' said the girl in a lilting voice, and she disappeared into the gloom.

A woman, tall and angular, appeared in the doorway and peered out into the driving rain.

'It's good to see you again, Will. Who's with you? Who is it?' The well-modulated English voice rose on a note of excitement and expectancy.

Gina felt Will's hand grip her elbow as he urged her forward up the steps.

'This is George, new chief cook and bottle-washer for the camp,' he announced firmly.

'Oh,' there was some disappointment in the woman's voice. 'I thought for a moment it was someone else. Come in, then.'

She turned into the house and they followed her into a wide hallway through an archway into a big pleasant room.

'It is Will, Drew, and he's brought a lad he calls George,' the woman was saying. The man lounging in a deep arm-chair burst out laughing as he looked past her at Gina and he was joined in his mirth by the other adolescent, who was a boy of about fourteen years of age. The woman swung round saw Gina and exclaimed,

'Oh! It isn't a boy at all.' Her blue eyes sparkling in her handsome big-featured face, which was somehow familiar. She rounded on Will. 'You mischievous devil,' she rebuked him. 'George, indeed! Now, what sort of a name is that for a wisp of a girl?' She smiled kindly at Gina.

'My name is Georgina,' said Gina, encouraged by that smile. 'Most of my friends call me Gina.'

'Which means you don't count Will amongst your friends, I should guess,' replied the woman. 'I'm Meg

Maxwell, Will's aunt, and this is my husband Andrew and my son Gordie.'

The man, who was tall and slim and had iron-grey hair, unfolded himself from his chair to greet Gina pleasantly and to shake hands with Will.

'We've been waiting for you for two days, now,' he said, in a soft lilting accent. 'What kept you?'

'The small business of finding someone to help Madge Anderson at the camp,' replied Will briefly. 'Who won today?' He settled down in a chair opposite to his host. Gordie immediately climbed on to the arm of the same chair to hang over him.

'Wales took a licking, I'm glad to say,' replied Andrew.

Meg touched Gina on the arm.

'Listen to them,' she murmured. 'Rugby Union fans, both of them.'

'Just like Oliver,' said Gina, who was still grappling with the fact that this woman was also Oliver's aunt and she had never heard of her before.

'Oliver?' queried Meg. Then light dawned in her eyes. 'Then you're *that* Georgina?'

'Yes. I was going to marry Oliver. He never told me about you.'

Meg's smile was wry.

'I'm not surprised. Ann, Will's mother, broke with us after she married again.'

'You are Oliver's father's sister, then?'

'Yes, I'm Geoff's sister. Much younger than he. I remember him as a young dashing officer, very gay and lively. Will is like him, or he used to be.' She glanced at her nephew rather anxiously. 'But there I go chattering on and you must be wanting a cup of tea. When did you eat last?'

Gina told her and Meg clucked her tongue disgustedly. This time the glance she sent in Will's direction was neither anxious nor affectionate.

'No wonder you look so pale and tired! Come upstairs and I'll show you where the bathroom is and the room

55

where you'll sleep tonight, and you can explain why you've come all this way with Will.'

Gina followed her from the room and up a wide open staircase. The very contemporary style of the house surprised her and she said so.

'I suppose you were expecting to stay in an old grey stone house with quaint dormer windows set in the roof, typically Scottish in design,' said Meg with a laugh. 'Well, you see, Andrew is an architect by profession and this house is his own design. We bought this land overlooking the loch a few years ago to get away from the city, and we love it. Nan, my daughter, is especially happy to live out here. She's horse-mad and we have two in the paddock nearby. By the way, where is she? I thought she went out to greet you.'

Gina explained and Meg smiled again.

'Your kitten will be in good hands, don't worry. Nan loves all animals. I'm surprised Will let you bring him.'

'I told him no Blue, no me, and he gave in,' said Gina coolly.

'You surprise me,' murmured Meg, giving her guest a slow assessing glance. 'He must have wanted you to come very badly. Will rarely gives in to anyone. If people won't go his way he usually ditches them. He can be very ruthless at times.'

'I'd noticed,' said Gina, following her hostess into a small bedroom decorated in bright colours and furnished with simple white furniture.

'Why did you come with him?' asked Meg.

'To prove to him that I'm not as soft as I look, and that I'm quite capable of cooking for twenty boys, more if necessary,' replied Gina, and again Meg looked at her curiously.

'I can see why Will thought you were soft,' she said, then added gravely, 'You won't let him down, will you, Gina? He's been let down rather badly. Another time might be once too often. I've noticed a tendency in him to become

56

rather withdrawn and dour lately. I'll leave you now. When you're ready, come down and we'll have a meal. We'll be able to chat afterwards because Andrew is taking Will to see a friend who is interested in sending his boys to the camp.'

When Gina eventually went downstairs feeling refreshed after a wash in unbelievably soft water, she found that Nan had come in and was trying to coax Blue to drink some milk from a saucer. The kitten was backed up against the kitchen wall, his back arched, his eyes wide.

'I found him in the stable. All the cats go in there because it's warm and cosy in the hay. He's lovely, so he is, but frightened of us,' said Nan, in her soft lilting voice. She was tall like her mother and her dark hair waved about her oval-shaped face which was lit by the blue eyes which were her inheritance from the Fox family.

Gina picked up the trembling kitten and stroked his damp fur.

'His name is Blue. Thank you for finding him.'

'You ... you're not Bridget, are you?' stammered Nan shyly, her eyes grave and questioning.

'Of course she isn't. She's Gina,' said Gordie in a whisper, glancing over his shoulder at his mother who was busy at the cooker.

'Who's Bridget?' asked Gina softly.

Two pairs of blue eyes regarded her steadily. Then Nan said quietly,

'She used to live here. She's the daughter of a friend of Mummy's who died. Bridget ran away.'

'Dinner is ready, so if you'd like to tell your father and Will, Gordie, Nan can take Gina through to the dining room,' said Meg, coming over to them. 'Leave the kitten here. I'll see that he gets something to eat.'

Recognising that Blue was amongst friends, Gina went with Nan and took her place at the dining-room table, where she was joined by Andrew and Will. The meal passed pleasantly, almost gaily. There was obviously good rapport between Will and his relatives and the conversation was scattered with family jokes.

As Gina ate she wondered about the terse whispered conversation which had taken place between herself and Nan. Who was Bridget, and why had she run away? And what had she to do with Will Fox?

When the meal was over the two men excused themselves to go and see the friend of Andrew who was interested in the adventure camp.

'You'll be all right, I hope,' Will said brusquely to Gina as he passed her on his way out of the room. 'Meg will look after you. In case you've gone to bed by the time I come back just remember that we want to make an early start again, about nine o'clock.'

She almost said 'Yes, sir,' and saluted him, Army fashion, but instead she confined herself to making a face at his retreating back.

'Don't you like Will?' asked the curious all-observant Nan, who thought the world of her grown-up cousin.

'Not much,' admitted Gina cautiously, thankful that Meg had left the room too.

'Bridget did. She thought he was a hero. That's why she ran after him and married him,' announced Nan.

Gina swallowed this amazing piece of information without a tremor, hoping she did not look as astonished as she felt.

'But her liking for him can't have lasted, because she ran away from him, so Mummy says,' continued Nan, who like many girls of her age was fascinated by the complicated relationships of adults. 'We haven't seen or heard from her since. Mum keeps hoping she'll turn up one day, but Daddy thinks she's dead.'

So that was why Meg's voice had risen in hope when she had noticed that Will had someone with him.

'When were they married?' asked Gina.

'Oh, years ago. About seven years, I suppose. Bridget was only eighteen. She went to London and then to Germany where Will was stationed then. She sent Mummy a photograph taken after they were married. It's upstairs. Mummy daren't have it down here in case Will sees it. Bridget was very pretty. She was always combing her hair and making up her face. I can remember watching her when I was little. Would you like to see the photo?'

'Perhaps you shouldn't take it from your mother's room,' Gina demurred. 'She might not want me to see it.'

'She won't mind. I expect she'll tell you all about Bridget because you're going to work for Will. I mean, it wouldn't do for you to fall in love with him, seeing how he's married, would it?'

Gina repressed a desire to inform Nan in her tartest tones that there wasn't the slightest possibility of her falling in love with Will, and the girl went off to get the photograph.

While Nan was away Meg reappeared and took Gina off to the living room where Gordie had settled on the floor in front of the television. Meg took out her knitting and, with a few questions, soon knew how Will had found Gina and had asked her to go and cook for him.

'I think I can understand the way his mind was working,' she said. 'He would be thinking it would be good for you to get away from Birmingham and the associations with Oliver. He would be understanding how you felt. He knows what it's like to lose a loved one.'

'You mean Bridget?' asked Gina.

'Has he told you about her?'

'Very little,' replied Gina, thinking of Will's terse comment about marriage and how it hadn't worked for him.

'It was such a shock to us when he wrote to tell us she'd run away from him,' said Meg. 'She had lived with us for about two years. I gave her a home when her mother, a good friend of mine, died quite suddenly of a heart attack. Her father disappeared into the blue years ago. And now it seems as if Bridget has inherited his vanishing tricks. I found her stubborn and very difficult to handle, but I as-

59

sumed that she was awkward because she had lost her mother at a crucial age. She was always wanting to stay out late at night. Then Will came here on leave. She thought he was wonderful and he took her out several times. He went back to Germany and soon afterwards Bridget ran away from here. I didn't hear from her until she wrote to say she'd met Will again and they were to be married.'

Meg sighed and took the photograph from Nan, who had come back into the room. She showed it to Gina, who gazed at the small pretty young woman with curling long hair and wide-set eyes, laughing up at a younger Will, in uniform, who looked rather serious on his wedding day.

'Hasn't he tried to find her?' she asked.

'Yes, whenever he could. Four years ago he left the Army and we didn't hear from him for a while. Then one day he turned up here to say he'd bought a place in the Highlands and that he intended to farm there. Not a word about Bridget, then or since. If I mention her he always changes the subject. We've no idea whether he found her or not. She could be dead for all we know.'

Meg concentrated on her knitting until she finished a row. Then she looked up and gazed at Gina with those clear observant eyes.

'Bridget wasn't unlike you,' she said. 'She was small and soft.'

Kitten-soft, Will had called her on their first meeting, thought Gina, and she wondered uneasily whether she had reminded him too of his wife.

But the warmth of the room was making her feel drowsy, and Meg noticed.

'I heard you being given orders about an early start tomorrow morning,' she said, with a humorous twitch to her lips, 'so I think you'd better go to bed. The journey has taken a lot out of you today, and Will won't have noticed. Basically he's a good person, but he tends to forget that others aren't as strong as he is. Now I've put the electric blanket on in your bed and I noticed Will had put your

60

cases in the room for you. I hope you've some warm night-wear for sleeping in when you get to the glen. It can be cold at night up there, even in May and June.'

Gina found the bed blissfully warm and she was soon asleep. She slept dreamlessly and heard nothing until some-one banged on the door hard enough to make it tremble.

'Eight-thirty, George. Want some breakfast before we go?' called a familiar masculine voice.

'Yes, please.'

'Then show a leg!'

The rain had stopped and the view from the bedroom window showed her the famous loch shimmering in pale sunlight with wreaths of pearly mist rising from it. In the distance, rising above the mist, she could see the sharp out-line of a snow-covered mountain peak shining against the sky.

Shivering in the cool air, she dressed quickly in warm woollen pants, a sweater and suede jacket. In the mirror her face looked surprisingly rested, the skin glowing faintly, the eyes bright and alert. Her hair was a tangle and she had time only to give it a few sweeps with the brush before tying it back with the chiffon scarf. No time for titivating with Will Fox waiting for her or he'd have no compunction about invading the room to hurry her along. A hard man who drove others hard and who had possibly driven his wife away from him.

Breakfast was a good wholesome meal at which the whole of the Maxwell family were present. Gina ate everything, remembering the hunger during the journey of the previous day. As soon as she had finished eating Will rose from the table saying it was time they left. Blue was placed in his basket under the canvas cover of the truck along with Gina's suitcases, and soon the truck was turning away from the house and Gina was waving goodbye to the assembled Maxwells.

The road north wound close beside the lake and offered fascinating glimpses of the smooth stretch of water from

61

beneath the down-curving branches of leafless larch trees or through the interlacing branches of dark pines. Feeling rested and comfortable, entranced by the serene beauty of scenery so different from that of her home county, Gina asked questions, and her companion, also in a better mood than on the previous day, answered her pleasantly and informatively. Soon she knew that the name of the snow-capped mountain rearing up on the opposite shores of the loch was Ben Lomond: that the names of all the islands she could see began with the word Inch; and as the loch narrowed and they twisted through a village called Tarbet, that the name meant small neck of land or isthmus and that the village was in fact on an isthmus created by the closeness of the head of Loch Long at that point to Loch Lomond.

With the lines of communication open Gina was encouraged to ask more questions about their destination, and learned that they were bound for a place called Glengorm.

'It means green or blue glen,' explained Will, 'and that describes it pretty well. In the summer it's all greens and blues.'

'How far is it from here?'

'Close on a hundred and twenty miles by road. If you'd like to see exactly where it is there's a map book underneath your seat. Look at the map showing the north-west of Scotland and you should be able to find it. It's in the area north of Ullapool.'

She did as he suggested and eventually found the glen, a narrow strip of green winding between masses of grey, which gave way to a strip of pale blue called Loch Gorm which opened on to the bigger mass of blue, representing the sea. Looking at the key to the map, Gina discovered that grey in all shades represented land above five hundred feet above sea level. There didn't seem to be any road of any importance leading to the glen or through it. Only a white line, which, according to the key, meant 'narrow country road, unsurfaced'.

'Why, it's miles away from anywhere,' she exclaimed. 'Whatever made you choose a place like that to live?'

'I didn't. It chose me,' was the laconic, bewildering reply.

'How?'

He was silent, seeming more interested in manoeuvring the vehicle round a bend on the outskirts of Crianlarich than in answering her question. Loch Lomond was now behind them and they faced the gradual pull up to Rannoch Moor.

Not receiving an answer, Gina glanced up from the map at Will, wondering whether to repeat her question, but the expression on his face prevented her from speaking. He was staring ahead, his eyes narrowed, his jaw ridged and rock-like, his mouth bitterly curved as he dealt with obviously unpleasant thoughts.

He spoke suddenly in a harsh voice.

'A few years ago, not long after I came out of the Army, I felt a great need to get away by myself. I decided to explore the Highlands alone. There I hoped to find glens, moors and mountains unblemished by dams, pylons and ski-lifts, and if I found any people, I hoped that they would be simple kindly souls untouched by the rat-race.'

He stopped speaking almost as abruptly as he'd begun, and Gina, surprised by the savagery of his outburst, was able to ask,

'Did you find what you hoped for?'

'Yes, I did. I found rest and peace, unchanging stability and a sense of the importance of old values, none of which I'd ever known before. I spent two days climbing in near-blizzard conditions in the area near Glengorm because an old man I'd met on the road said that I would see paradise from the top of a certain mountain. I was on the top of Ben Searg when the cloud broke suddenly. Sunlight appeared and glinted on a sheet of water. It was like a momentary glimpse of paradise, of a promised land. I hurried down the mountain and made my way towards the loch. That night I slept in my tent beside the loch in a copse of birch trees to the sound of a torrent roaring in the glen.'

He paused again, and this time Gina didn't ask any questions. She was too busy grappling with yet another new aspect of Will Fox. Why had he found it necessary to get away alone? Had the disappearance of his young wife affected him more deeply than he had cared to admit to anyone?

'Next day,' he continued more quietly, 'when I awoke and looked out not a ripple broke the smooth blue surface of the loch, which reflected silent white hills and the dark ruins of an old tower built on a promontory. Near the tower I found a house, deserted but in good repair. There were fields around it that had once been tilled. In a state of great excitement I decided I would live there and farm. As soon as I could I went down to Ullapool and enquired about the place. It was for sale—house, fields, moors and half a mountain, the whole glen, in fact. In the grip of a strange fascination I made an offer for it. It was accepted immediately. I've lived there ever since.'

'How long?'

'Four years this coming Easter. Eighteen months by myself, except for Lachie Munro, who is the only crofter in the glen. The rest of the time Gavin Anderson has been there with me setting up the buildings for the adventure camp.' He chuckled reminiscently. 'We had a great time erecting the huts which I bought at an auction. We finished them just before the first batch of youngsters arrived last year.'

'What do you do with the boys?' she asked.

'Try to pass on to them skills which have given me so much pleasure in life.'

'What are they?'

'Climbing, camping, sailing, canoeing, fishing, forestlore, also simple rules for survival in the wilderness. That reminds me—I didn't ask you. Have you any other skill besides cooking?'

Gina thought of the dinghy sailing which she'd done

since she was ten, sharing the boat with her brothers. She hadn't done much since she'd met Oliver, but she knew it was a skill which she would never lose.

'I can sail a dinghy,' she offered diffidently. 'Luke, my eldest brother, and I once won a junior championship.'

He flashed her an interested glance.

'Good for you,' he murmured. 'You'll be of more use than I'd hoped. You can help out with the sailing instruction when the weather is suitable.'

Gina forbore to remind him that she would not be staying very long in Glengorm, only until Gavin's wife was able to cope again.

She was finding that she had no wish to fight with Will Fox this morning. Knowledge of his failed marriage was making her view him quite differently. He wasn't just a rough, tough ex-soldier accustomed to giving orders and getting his own way. He was a man who had loved and lost, who had made a mistake and had paid for it.

His mood also was softer, as if he was feeling the influence of the place he had made his home. He was less relentless in his desire to reach it and even condescended to stop at the Bridge of Orchy. For a while they leaned together on the ancient stone structure watching the river swirling down from Loch Tulle, comparing it with that other more placid river they had watched in Stratford. The air was cold and sharp but invigorating. The brown moors were silent, stretching away endlessly to the distant mountains. No traffic passed them. They had all that Sunday morning to themselves. They could have been the only people alive in the world.

Lunch was taken leaning against the truck where it was parked on a grassy sward beside another river further north, beyond the ramparts of Ben Nevis. Blue, sniffing and curious, trampled the grass happily. There were few signs of spring even though the sunshine was warm.

The afternoon was spent travelling deeper and deeper into the mountains along a winding road, past solitary crofts and remote dark forests. There was very little traffic, although Will assured Gina that the same road would be busy with caravans and cars in the summer. The lack of traffic and of people gave Gina a sense of aloneness and insignificance, which was increased by the strange shapes of some of the mountains.

By the time the sun was slipping down the sky she was a willing prisoner to the image of the Highlands as presented to her that day of April. There was enchantment in the landscape as burns, forests and mountains unfolded before her when the road wound on past Achnasheen and Loch a Chroisg, through the lifting, lilting land.

When the sun had gone the light lingered long in the west, but darkness came inevitably and there were still many miles to go. Steadily the truck ground onwards. Hunger gurgled noisily in Gina's stomach and her head nodded. She felt rather than saw the last bend in the road because she was pitched towards Will and then away from him again. Then they were gliding downwards towards the faint shimmer of water. She could just make out the bulk of a tower against the clear starlit sky. She saw a white house gleaming amongst the delicate tracery of branches. The vehicle stopped, the engine was cut and in the silence she could hear the lowing of a cow from a barn.

There were no lights shining from the house and she sensed an uneasiness in her companion as he sat still for a moment.

'I wonder where everyone is,' he said at last, and opened the door on his side.

He jumped out. Gina left the truck more slowly and stiffly. The air was cold and crisp and she could hear water lapping on an unseen shore.

She was aware that Will had gone to the house and was opening the porch door. She heard him yell rudely, his voice abrasive.

'Gavin, Madge! Where the hell are you?'

Only the echo of his own voice answered him. He disappeared and Gina waited. From the back of the truck came the inevitable pitiable mewing of the kitten. Remembering how he had run away the previous evening Gina decided to wait until Will came back to her before she attempted to take the kitten out of the truck. She felt the would like a little light on the subject before she made any move.

Standing there in the starlit dark, listening to the soft lap of water on a shore, hearing the faint soughing of the wind in the branches of trees she was aware of a strange dread forming in her mind. Where were Gavin and Madge Anderson? Why hadn't they answered Will's call? Why were there no lights in the house?

There was probably a perfectly reasonable answer to her questions, but she could not help recalling Meg Maxwell's anxious remark about Will having been let down rather badly once and that the next time he was let down might be once too often and have a detrimental effect on him. Was it possible that the Andersons had let him down?

Gina shivered and would have given anything in that moment to have been back in Birmingham in her own comfortable flat instead of standing in the damp darkness of a Highland glen waiting for the reappearance of the man who had brought her there.

CHAPTER THREE

LIGHT flickered out from one of the ground floor windows of the house. Gina guessed it came from an oil lamp which had just been lit. The faint glow grew in strength as she waited and watched.

Then Will spoke from the doorway. His voice was loud and harsh, shattering the silence and making her jump.

'Aren't you coming in?' he barked.

'Yes, yes, of course,' she called back, thinking he didn't sound very welcoming. 'But I'd like to get Blue out first. I can't see a thing.'

'You'll have to get used to the darkness. We don't have street lighting in the glen,' he replied sardonically.

Gina's heart sank a little. His softer, more kindly mood had evaporated. Once more he was the tough Army captain issuing orders. He reached under the canvas cover for Blue. swore and withdrew his hand quickly as the kitten scratched him.

'Here, you get him out,' he growled at her. 'I'll take the cases.'

Blue felt soft and warm. Gina was comforted by the feel of her pet who was a familiar friend in that unfamiliar place.

Cautiously she followed Will along a path to the door of the house and stepped into a porch and then through another door into a narrow hallway. From there they went into a room from which the light came.

It was a big room with bare stone walls which had been painted a cheerful yellow. The wooden floor had been sanded and varnished and it was scattered with bright rugs. The furniture was mixed; comfortable armchairs set about a stone fireplace; a big roll-topped desk; a pretty oval-shaped gate-legged table on which the oil lamp hissed and flared.

Gina stood hesitantly, hugging Blue close to her, rubbing her cheek against his fur as Will set down her cases beside the desk. He glanced across at her and his mouth quirked sardonically.

'I'm beginning to feel a little sorry for Noll—in retrospect, of course,' he murmured.

'Why?'

'He had to compete with that kitten for your love.'

'He didn't have to do anything of the sort,' she retorted indignantly, surprised by this sudden attack. 'I loved him just as much as I love Blue.'

The sardonic twist became more apparent.

'Just as much? Not more than?' he queried jeeringly. 'Then I reckon Noll is better off where he is. At least he won't suffer disillusionment finding out that you loved him only as much as you love your pet.'

'That isn't what I meant at all,' she flared. 'I loved Oliver in a totally different way from the way I love Blue. He didn't have to compete with anyone. Anyway, he wasn't like you. I would never have had to run away from him as your wife ran away from you.'

The words were no sooner out of her mouth than she regretted them. She didn't usually go in for wounding people deliberately. She couldn't think why she'd said them except that there had been an overriding need to retaliate, to hurt him as much as he seemed intent on hurting her.

His eyes were a hard soulless blue, making her doubt whether it was possible to hurt him.

'So Meg talked, did she?' he said coolly. 'Just as well, really. Saves me the trouble, and maybe it'll stop you from getting any sloppy ideas. And now to find out why Gavin and Madge have skipped. There should be a note somewhere.'

Her heart sinking even lower Gina followed him out of the room because he took the lamp with him. Shadows pranced on the walls of the hallway as they went down it into another big room, which was obviously the kitchen. It was well equipped with cupboards and cooking facilities and in the middle of the floor was a long table with benches on either side. Obviously the campers ate their meals there.

The note was on the table, a single sheet of paper held down by a water jug. Gina looked round the room while Will read it, not daring to watch the expression on his face change.

The sound of the paper being scrunched by a hand drew her attention and, fascinated, she watched Will's long fingers curled round the note with a viciousness which frightened her. She expected him to swear, but all he said was,

'I might have guessed. The little. . .!'

She never heard what he intended to call either Madge or Gavin because he didn't finish the sentence, but she guessed it wasn't complimentary.

'What's wrong?' she asked hesitantly. His face was dark, his eyes looking paler and harder than ever. He tossed the crumpled note on to the table.

'Read it,' he barked, and went out of the room.

Still clutching Blue, Gina picked up the note and straightened it out. It was written in a rather schoolboyish scribble.

Dear Will,

I've had to take Madge down to her parents' home. She feels she can stand this place no longer. Personally, I think that it's her condition which is making her hypersensitive to atmosphere, but there's nothing I can do about it. If I don't take her away she says she'll leave me. I'd like to say that we'd be coming back once the child is born, but somehow I don't think that will happen.

Sorry to let you down. I hope you'll understand why I've had to put her first. It was good while it lasted, Will, for me at any rate.

Good luck.
Gavin.

So her intuitive feeling that the Andersons had deserted Will had been right, thought Gina, as she placed the note back on the table. Once again Will had been let down. They must have gone while his back had been turned because they had been unable to tell him to his face that they wanted to leave. In order to get her own way with her husband Madge had used a weapon Gavin had known that Will would appreciate. She had threatened to leave him if he did not do as she wished. No wonder Will had been tempted to call Madge rude names!

Instead of standing there clutching her pet and shivering she should be showing some spirit and doing something to help soften the blow which the desertion of the Andersons must be to Will. Meg Maxwell had been afraid of how another let-down might affect him. Well, the new cook and bottle-washer was going to make sure that it brought him nothing but benefits.

Setting Blue down on the floor, Gina went over to the cooker. It was big and shiny and possessed several burners on one of which was a kettle. She filled the kettle with water. Instinctively she found matches and the gas storage cylinder. She turned on the regulator to release the gas from the container, then turned on one of the burners and lit it before placing the kettle on it. Soon she was searching cupboards for food and cooking equipment.

Her weariness evaporated miraculously as she worked and soon she was humming to herself as she pottered about. Blue was silenced with some tinned milk and by the time Will returned to the kitchen, after bringing in all the luggage from the truck, the table was set at one end for two people. The smell of soup being heated and something savoury being cooked in the oven made the kitchen seem the homely, welcoming place it should be.

Hearing Gina humming a tune he often whistled himself, Will grinned at her.

'I never thought I'd hear someone as prudish as you singing a song like that,' he teased her. 'Do you know what it's

71

about?'

'Seduction?' she guessed, colour flaming wildly in her cheeks as she met his amused glance. He looked less violent now, she was relieved to see.

'In the nicest possible sense,' he replied, 'and with a happy ending. The food smells good. How soon can we eat?'

'In about fifteen minutes. I've made some tea. I expect you could do with a cup. I know I could,' she said.

'After that blow beneath the belt from the Andersons I think I'm in need of something stronger,' he remarked, going over to a cupboard and taking down a bottle of whisky. He poured some into a glass, then leaned against the table and sipped some of it, and watched her pouring tea.

'You look very much at home,' he commented, noting how the effort of preparing the meal had loosened some of her hair from the chiffon scarf which tied it back, so that corkscrew ringlets dangled tantalisingly about her flushed cheeks.

The expression in his eyes disturbed her, making her suddenly very aware of her position alone with him in his house miles away from anywhere, preparing his evening meal as if she were his wife.

She looked away from that disturbing blue gaze and squeaked a question from a throat which was dry.

'What are you going to do now that Gavin and Madge have gone?'

'Carry on. What else can I do? With twenty lively youngsters and their two social workers arriving tomorrow I can hardly change everything now. Anyway, you're here, and a good cook on the premises means that half the battle is won. I can manage the instruction courses myself and we can organise the lads to help with the washing up.' He paused and gave her a strange underbrowed glance. 'Unless it's in your mind to do a disappearing act, too,' he tacked on.

Bitterness made his voice harsh again and etched lines

round his mouth, but she noticed there was no self-pity there.

'I'm not in the habit of letting people down,' she returned loftily, looking at him down her straight shapely nose. 'I said I'd help you out until...'

'Until Madge was able to cope again,' he reminded her drily. 'But you see Madge won't be coming back, ever, and there's the camp in May to get through as well as the summer camps, and all those letters to answer from hopeful youngsters wanting to come and cupboards to stock with food.'

She sent him a wide-eyed glance. His gaze met hers steadily. He was not appealing to her for himself. He was making her feel that if she didn't stay she would be letting down all sorts of people she had never met.

'I'll stay until you find someone else to help you, no longer,' she said.

His mouth twitched and dark eyelashes hid his eyes as he looked down at his drink.

'Good for you, George,' he said softly. 'Now I know where I stand.'

'But what about other help? Who will take Gavin's place? Do you know anyone else who would be willing to come and live here?' she asked.

'I know of someone who is interested,' he replied vaguely, and tossed off the remains of his whisky. Then he gave her another penetrating stare. 'No one, I repeat no one, is irreplaceable in this life, George. Neither a partner, nor a wife, nor yet a fiancé.'

That stung. Again her wide glance flew to his and stayed briefly, only to fall away before the intensity of his. Her distress must have shown in her face because he put out a hand and touched her gently on the cheek. She flinched away from his touch and turned on him like an angry cat. He smiled gently.

'All right, kitten,' he soothed. 'My intention was only to comfort you—I know you believe that no one can ever take the place of Oliver. But that isn't true. Someone else will come along one day and the old chemistry will start working and before you know where you are you'll be wanting to share his bed . . .'

'Never!' she spat at him. 'Anyway, that isn't why I wanted to marry Oliver. We both agreed that the physical aspect of marriage was the least important part. We wanted to marry for other reasons too.'

He raised his eyebrows and whistled jeeringly.

'Did you now,' he drawled, and devilment danced in his eyes. 'How very civilised of you both! I had a feeling that might have been the way of it. You're remarkably unawakened for a young woman who was about to be married only ten days ago. Far be it from me to criticise Noll's methods of wooing you. I suppose he knew what he was doing. After all, he was a doctor.' He sniffed and jerked his head in the direction of the cooker. 'Something seems to require your attention over there. I'll go and wash my hands and hope that when I come back the grub will be ready to eat. I'm famished.'

He left the room again whistling that tantalisingly familiar tune which, she realised now, she had been humming to herself. Hand to the cheek he had touched, which seemed hotter than the other, she attended to the soup which had been about to boil over. She wondered if she would ever learn to avoid falling into the traps Will Fox set for her to fall into during the course of conversation. He set them, she was sure, for his own amusement because her innocent serious replies made him laugh. How on earth was she going to work for and live with him for most of the summer?

Live with him! The words screamed through her mind like warning. That was just what she was going to do. She was going to live alone with him in this house without the chaperonage of the Andersons, unless there was another house where she could live.

While they were eating she approached the new problem in a round about way, wary of any scoffing remarks he might make. She asked first of all where the Andersons had lived.

'Here, in this house, on a temporary basis. Gav was going to build a house, but he kept putting it off. I think he knew as much as I did that Madge wouldn't stick it out here,' he replied tersely.

'Did you sleep in one of the huts?' she asked diffidently.

He looked up, puzzled.

'No, why should I? This is my house, and it's big enough to house three families, let alone one. They had the third floor. I sleep on the second floor.'

'But when the campers are here don't you sleep in the bunkhouse then?'

He gave her a rather pitying glance.

'Look, George, some of the lads and lasses who come are almost twenty. None of them is younger than fifteen. Even if they come without an adult leader, I reckon they're quite old enough to sleep in the bunkhouse without supervision. Now, come clean and tell me what's really on your mind. You're not very good at a flank attack.'

'Living alone here with you,' she gulped hastily, and her face burned red again.

He stared at her for a few seconds, obviously taken aback.

'I'm not sure how to take that remark. Seems to me you're casting aspersions on my character,' he said in frost-bitten tones.

'I'm sorry,' she muttered. 'I didn't mean to. I just thought it might look odd to other people, you and I living in the same house when we're not married or anything.'

Under the dagger-swift glance of his eyes her spirit quailed and her voice trailed away to silence.

'I see,' he said, and although there was still a sprinkling of frost, his voice was slightly warmer. He rubbed his chin reflectively with one hand. 'Without Gavin and Madge here, there might be gossip. Is that what you're getting at?'

75

She nodded and couldn't prevent her face from flaming again.

'Well, there's nothing we can do about that,' he replied calmly. 'I must say the thought hadn't occurred to me and I can assure you that it won't occur to our nearest neighbour, Lachie Munro. But now that you mention it I can see that it might create difficulties later.' He paused and frowned, rubbing his chin again, gazing with narrowed eyes at nothing, as if a new thought had struck him. Then he shrugged and looked at her. 'Not to worry, George. If anyone is unpleasant I'll deal with them. Of course, if you'd really prefer to sleep in the bunkhouse, you can, but don't expect me to move out of here.'

She hesitated, not knowing what to say. His calm attitude was making her feel as if she had made a fuss about nothing. His eyes had begun to twinkle again as he noticed her hesitation and she wished she'd kept her mouth shut in the first place.

'No,' he cautioned, 'don't decide yet. Wait until I've shown you the room where you're going to sleep. Madge decorated it all ready for the new cook. I've put your luggage up there and it's a flight of stairs above mine, if that makes you feel any easier. The bunkhouse is all right, but a bit rough, and once the campers come you'd have no privacy there.'

She went with him meekly up the stairs to the third floor. There were two large attic bedrooms, one of which had been the Andersons'. Will led her into the other and in the soft light cast by the oil lamp which he placed on the high Victorian chest of drawers she could see that the room had been recently decorated.

'Well? What do you think? Here, or the bunkhouse?' he asked.

'Here,' she muttered, avoiding his mocking gaze.

'I thought that would be the way of it,' he remarked drily.

She pushed her hand across her forehead in a gesture of

76

weariness. The bed under its old-fashioned patchwork cover looked inviting, and she longed for nothing more than to climb into it and sleep.

As she lowered her hand Oliver's diamond ring which she still wore on the third finger of her left hand caught the light and flashed brightly. Will's eyes narrowed and hardened when he saw it.

'You're tired,' he observed brusquely. 'I'll get the sheets for the bed. You may as well turn in now.'

His concern surprised her. She had thought he didn't notice when anyone was tired.

'But the dishes——' she began.

'I'll do them,' he replied curtly.

He left the room, returning within a few seconds with clean sheets and pillow slips. He was followed by Blue, who entered stealthily, ears cocked and tail on high.

'What shall I do about Blue?' asked Gina.

'Do you really want to know what *I* think you should do with him?' he asked, looking down at the kitten menacingly.

'No, no,' she said quickly.

'Then don't ask foolish questions. He's your responsibility, not mine, and as long as I don't find him curled up on *my* bed I don't care a hang where he sleeps. Good night, George.'

He went out closing the door behind him, but the old-fashioned latch had hardly settled into place than it lifted again and he put his head around the jamb. Devilment was back in his eyes, blue and twinkling.

'I'm afraid there's no lock on this door, but I know of a trick which I've found useful in the past, when I haven't wanted to be disturbed.'

He came in, closed the door, strode across to an old chair with a tall ladderback, picked it up and going back to the door tilted the chair against it so that the top rung of the ladderback rested under the latch.

'It won't keep a determined intruder out, but it will slow

him down considerably,' he said with a grin. Then lifting the chair away, he opened the door and went out again, the grin still wickedly flickering as he murmured, 'G'night. Sleep well.'

She did sleep well, worn out with the journey as well as the strange emotional upheaval coming north with Will Fox had caused within her. She did not wake until the flat of a hand hit the old door, making it tremble and causing Blue to jump up on to the bed, spitting and growling with fright.

'Show a leg George!' Will sounded as vigorous as usual. 'It's seven-thirty. Breakfast is ready and this is the last time I cook it this week. If you're not down in ten minutes I'll come and drag you out of bed!'

The air felt chilly to the end of her nose and she was reluctant to move from the warm bed, but she couldn't risk having him come in and pull her from the bed as he had threatened.

No wonder Bridget had run away from him if that was the sort of treatment she had had to put up with, she thought, and then she reprimanded herself for her unkind thought. Will was probably just as capable of treating someone he loved as gently as the next man was, and considering the circumstances perhaps it was best if he were rough with her.

Blue was rubbing against the door asking to be let out, so, flinging back the bedclothes, Gina braved the chilliness of her first morning in the Highlands and hurried to open the door. The kitten slid through the opening and padded away downstairs.

Opening the flower-printed curtains, Gina gazed out. Four slender silver birches, their trunks gilded by morning sunlight, made a frame for a picture of winter-bleached moorland, sloping down to a blue loch beyond which a mountain reared, a perfect cone topped with sunlit icing where the snow reflected the morning light. While she stared entranced by the wild alien landscape, a pair of swans flew over the loch and slid heavily into the water, spattering it with silver ripples.

Excited by the sight of them, she dressed quickly and went downstairs. Will was sitting at the table eating and looking at some letters. Gina went over to the oven and took out her breakfast, then sat down at the place set for her.

'I've just seen two swans land on the lake—I mean the loch,' she announced, unable to keep the excitement out of her voice.

His reaction surprised her. He looked up sharply, his eyes widening.

'Say that again,' he ordered.

She repeated what she had said and added, 'Is that so unusual? You look very surprised.'

With an obvious effort he collected himself and shrugged.

'Just a sign that spring is on its way,' he murmured evasively.

'Oh, it does come here, then? I was beginning to wonder whether it ever came when I saw the snow on the mountain top,' she said drily.

'You'll find other signs, if you care to look,' he replied with a grin.

'Such as?'

'Flowers hiding in warm sheltered crannies.'

'Oh, what sort?' Gina was delighted. She glanced at the bare formica top of the table and imagined it covered with a pretty cloth and an arrangement of spring flowers in the centre.

'Primroses. When you've finished eating, grab a jacket and I'll show you round the place. I might even show you where the primroses are.'

Outside the air was sharp but fresh. There was no sound other than that of cold water running here and there through rocks and lank brown heather or lapping at the shores of the loch. Will showed her the copse where he had

79

camped the first time he had come to the glen and made her listen for the sound of the torrent inland, which had lulled him to sleep.

'Just four years ago,' he said. 'There's quite a difference in the place since then. Come and see the bunkhouses.'

On their way to the timber huts which were situated on a plateau of land close to the lochside to the right of the house, they passed a barn. A tall man with a shock of greying hair who was wearing denim dungarees over a thick woollen shirt appeared in the doorway.

'Good morning, Lachie,' Will greeted him. 'This is George. She's come to cook for the campers.'

'Good day to you, miss,' said the other man. His round innocent blue eyes had a slightly dazed look in them as he regarded her pants.

'When did the Andersons leave?' asked Will.

'I'm thinking it would be a day or two after you left,' said Lachie, wrinkling his forehead. 'She was after giving him no peace. She'll be no loss to the glen.'

'Perhaps you're right,' said Will. 'But I shall miss Gavin.'

'Aye, he was a grand lad. It's a pity, so it is, that he was caught,' murmured Lachie, who was still furtively eyeing Gina. 'Have you been seeing the swans?'

'Not yet. But George has. When did they come?' Will sounded a little uneasy at the mention of the big white birds.

'The evening before last, just as the sun was setting. Ach, I couldn't believe my own eyes,' said Lachie, and chuckled suddenly, the expression in his eyes now decidedly impish as he looked from Gina to Will and then back to Gina again. 'I should have known you'd be bringing a bonny lass with you.'

He turned back into the barn, and they continued on their way to the bunkhouse. Will led the way, striding quickly, a frown on his face.

'What did he mean by saying he should have known

80

you'd be bringing me with you?' asked Gina as soon as she could catch up with him. She had read that the Highlanders often believed in second sight and she wondered whether Lachie possessed the ability to see into the future.

'He was referring to an ancient legend about the glen,' said Will curtly. 'You'll find that Highlanders usually have some tale to tell about the places in which they live. They use them to explain anything which is strange about the place. It's best to listen to them with a grain of salt. I've no time for such stories myself.'

No, you've no time for them, but this one has disturbed you for some reason, thought Gina, grimacing at his broad back as he opened the door of the nearest bunkhouse, and she decided that she would ask Lachie Munro as soon as she could to tell her the legend of the swans.

Although there was a certain amount of pride in Will's bearing as he showed her the bunkhouses with their rows of camp beds, showers, wash basins and drying rooms, which he had erected with the help of Gavin and Lachie, the enthusiasm with which he had set out had waned. His withdrawal became more and more noticeable as they returned to the house. His mind was obviously not on what he was doing and he had forgotten to show her where she would find primroses.

Perhaps it was just as well, thought Gina with a sigh as she looked round the clean well-equipped kitchen after she had finished clearing up the breakfast dishes. After all, she was not there to decorate the place, as Will had pointed out, nor to soften the house's uncompromising austerity and masculinity. She was there as a volunteer to help out until another partner could be found to help run the camps.

After a midday meal which Lachie shared with them, Will went off to Lochinvie to collect post which might have arrived while he had been away. He didn't invite Gina to accompany him, but gave her instructions about making sure the beds in the bunkhouse were ready and to prepare dinner for the hungry youths expected that evening.

When she had done all she could in the way of preparation Gina realised that Blue was missing. Going outside, she found the afternoon was mild and sunny. Down the slope from the house the loch dimpled under the caress of a slight breeze and the dark tower had lost some of its dour aspect. aspect.

She called to Blue and wandered down the path to the loch. Near the small curving beach of shingle the two swans sat. At her approach they reared their necks and hissed, then waddled down to the water and took off to swim sedately away.

From high above her head Gina heard the plaintive but unmistakable cry of her kitten. Looking upwards at the tower, she saw a cheeky blue-grey face peeping out of an opening in the ruin.

'Oh, Blue, you naughty kitten! How did you get there? Come down at once!' she called.

Blue merely put his head on one side and looked mischievous. Gina approached the tower more closely.

'Come down, Blue,' she ordered.

'Do not be worrying about the wee cat, miss,' said a voice nearby, and looking round, she saw Lachie sitting on a rough stone bench near the entrance to the tower. He was enjoying the sunshine and quiet smoke of his pipe. 'If you'd be after sitting down for a wee while the cat will come down in its own good time,' he added. 'Ach, it's a lovely day, so it is, and we're in no hurry, no hurry at all.'

Listening to the lazy drone of his voice and seeing the expression of permanent pleasure on his lined weather-beaten face, Gina guessed that Lachie had never been in a hurry in his life.

Accepting the invitation to dawdle with him for a while, she sat down on the bench next to him and leaned back against the rough stone of the tower. The sunshine was warm on her skin and when she closed her eyes it glowed behind her eyelids.

'Aye, it's a free and easy life, so it is,' continued Lachie, his voice making slow music in the soft air. 'I can shoot a deer if it comes on my croft and I can fish in the burns and in the sea. If I need extra money I can come and work for Will Fox or go to Ullapool to mend fish boxes. You'll be knowing the old Gaelic saying, perhaps?'

'No. I know nothing about the Gaels,' said Gina humbly.

'Then there's a lot for you to be learning,' he said. 'It goes like this: "When God made time he made plenty of it." Remember that and you'll never be suffering from indigestion,' said Lachie wisely. 'And now you'll be telling which part of England you come from.'

She told him, and then listened to a long story about the time he had visited Birmingham during the second world war.

'And is that big market place, the Bull Ring, still there?' he asked, coming to the end of his tale.

'Yes, but it's all been rebuilt since you were there. You wouldn't recognise it now,' she replied.

'And there'll be too much traffic, I'm thinking, and people in a hurry,' he murmured. 'Ach, you're better off living here where it's quiet and no one is in a hurry, not even Will. For all he has the ways of a conqueror, he can take it easy and slow when he's a mind to it.'

Easy and Slow. That was the title of the folk song which Will whistled. But the song wasn't about work. It was about the slow, sly seduction of a young woman, suggestive in its lilting melody and phrasing. Yes, she could imagine Will Fox conquering a woman by easy, slow methods if he found his usual direct method of attack failing to win him what he wanted.

'How long have you lived in the glen?' she asked Lachie.

'Since I was a young man. I took over my grandfather's croft just after the war.'

'Are you married?'

'I was, but my wife went away. The glen cannot hold a woman, or it couldn't until two days ago.'

'Oh? Why is that?' asked Gina, her interest caught.

83

Lachie pointed with the stem of his pipe at the swans which were still sailing slowly on the water.

'They have come back after being away for almost three hundred years,' he intoned.

'But I thought they came here each spring?' said Gina.

'There has been no swan seen in Glengorm since the chief of the Macneal clan lived in this tower,' he replied.

'When was that?'

'In the seventeenth century. He was a soldier too, fighting for King Charles the Second. Once when he came back to his inheritance, which included this glen, all of that mountain and the big castle on the other side of it, he brought a young bride with him. She came from the south, like you. Lovely she was, but as shy and timid as a roedeer. She preferred living in the tower here to living in the castle. She liked to feed the swans when she felt lonely, and she was often lonely because she was barren and bore no children and her husband the chief of the clan was often away.'

Lachie paused to relight his pipe. Gina, enthralled by the story which she guessed was the legend to which Will had referred, watched the swans and imagined the slight figure of a young woman dressed in a long gown, with ringlets of hair falling over her shoulders, standing on the shore throwing pieces of bread to the big birds.

'Then one day she disappeared,' said Lachie, his pipe going to his satisfaction. 'In the autumn it was, when the leaves were gold and russet and the heather turned brown. She went when the swans flew south. All winter she was away. The people of the glen said she had gone with the swans she loved, back to her own place and people, turning into a swan maiden and flying with the birds. They said she would come back when the swans returned in the spring. They said that to comfort the chief, who was brokenhearted when he could not find his dear one.'

'Did he ever find her?' asked Gina in an awed whisper. She was finding the similarity of the story to the little she knew about Will Fox's marriage rather disconcerting.

'No. All that winter he waited, and when the spring came he watched, but the swans never came, nor did his wife. The next year it was the same, and in all the years that followed neither his wife nor the swans were seen in the glen again. After a while the chief married again, but his new wife would not stay in the glen. Gradually all the women left the crofts, and since then no woman has been able to stay in the glen. My own grandfather did not take over his croft until his wife had died, and my father did not dare to live here because his wife would not come.'

'What a strange story,' murmured Gina. 'But surely there was some reasonable explanation for the young woman's disappearance. Perhaps she drowned in the loch, or something like that?'

'She flew away with the swans,' said Lachie stubbornly. 'And the glen has been cursed ever since then.'

'Are there any of the Macneal's descendants living near here?' asked Gina, deciding not to argue with him.

'Ach, yes. Mistress Macneal comes to the castle at Easter and stays there until the autumn. The rest of the time she's away in some warm climate, Florida, or the Mediterranean, or some such place. She's the chief of the clan now, since her old father died, leaving no male heir. She married a star-spangled Scot for his money and persuaded him to change his name to Macneal.'

'Star-spangled Scot?' repeated Gina with a laugh. 'What do you mean?'

'He's an American with Scottish ancestors and a Scottish name,' replied Lachie, imperturbable as ever. 'Aye, the Macneals did well when the chief married him.'

'Do they still own the glen?'

'Ach, no. Will owns it. When the Macneals were poor, a while back, they started to sell off the land. This part was bought by a man called Henderson who hoped to turn it into his country estate. He built the house yonder and called it White Lodge, but his wife would not stay, no more than

Madge Anderson would. She said she felt the glen didn't want her, that the spirit of the young bride was pushing her out.'

'You mean she saw the ghost of the woman?' exclaimed Gina.

'Aye.' Lachie puffed contentedly at his pipe.

'Did Madge say she had seen it too?'

'It suited her to say she had,' said Lachie drily. 'But do not be worrying about it. You'll not see it because you've come with the swans, and the curse says that no woman will rest in Glengorm until the swans come back in the spring-time when the true mistress of the master of the glen returns.'

Gina looked closely at his long-jawed face. He seemed quite serious and his innocent blue eyes returned her gaze openly.

'You're not sure whether you believe me or not, are you lass?' Lachie queried softly.

'No, I'm not. Who is master of the glen now?'

'Will Fox. He bought it from the Henderson family.'

No wonder Will had looked at her sharply when she had said she had seen the swans that morning. No wonder he had been disturbed by their return.

'Lachie, do you know what the name of the Macneal's wife was?' she asked.

'I mind she was called Bridie, the Scottish version of the name Bridget, common enough in the Highlands and Islands. Look now, there's your wee cat. Wasn't I after telling you he would be coming to join you if you didn't hurry him? Ach, it's a fine wee pussy you have there, and you'll have to be taking care of him and not letting him roam too far, and him not used to the land yet.'

If he was still disturbed by the return of the swans to Glengorm, Will gave no sign of it on his return from Lochinvie. He brought many letters, applications he said from people wishing to attend the camps in the summer and he expected her help in going through them and answering them.

Not long after his return the first group of campers arrived, having walked over the moors from Ullapool as part of the adventure course. Most of them were boys between the ages of fourteen and sixteen, excited by their first visit to the Highlands and grateful for the meal to which they helped themselves in the kitchen. Another group including some girls followed half an hour later.

The youngsters were accompanied by two social workers; one was a burly bearded young man called Steve Harris who was the outdoor projects officer of the youth association to which the youngsters belonged, and the other was a slim fair young woman named Janet Fines.

Janet confided in Gina that she was really a teacher of art in a school in Glasgow but that she gave some of her free time to the youth association which had been organised in the slum area in order to help youngsters, disorientated by their removal from old condemned tenements, to new housing estates.

'How do you help them?' enquired Gina.

'By teaching them pottery amongst other skills, taking groups of seven to eight of them after school is over. The classes serve a dual purpose. Apart from learning a skill they talk to me, and that's a contact with them, and I learn to know them and to understand something of what they're up against, the despondency of decay and demolition. This place is a marvellous contrast to the place where they live at present and we're lucky that Captain Fox has made it available to them. I'm sorry though that Madge had to give up, and I hope her desertion won't set him against social workers as a whole,' said Janet anxiously.

'He may not have very kindly feelings towards her personally,' replied Gina, 'but I don't think he's the sort of person to allow her behaviour to prevent him from doing something which he considers worthwhile.'

'I hope you're right. Anyway he has you to help him now. I must say that meal was very good. If you're going to feed us all like that during the next two weeks I'm going to put on weight,' laughed the lively, energetic Janet.

During the next few days Gina worked harder than at any time in her life. Up early every morning, obeying the summons of Will's hand on her bedroom door, she cooked twenty-six breakfasts, then cleared away and washed up. After that she prepared the food for the evening meal and also for the packed lunches which the campers took with them on the various expeditions. Admittedly she had help, but there were times when she thought nostalgically of the various electrical gadgets her mother had possessed to assist in the preparation of meals.

One evening half way through the camp, feeling particularly tired as she tidied up after finishing all the preparations for the next day, her mind wandered to the strange legend of the swans as told to her by Lachie Munro. It was probably only coincidence that the name of the wife of the Macneal who had once been master of the glen had been Bridie, the Highland version of Bridget, but it could be enough of a coincidence to raise Will's hopes about the possible return of his own wife, now that the swans had come back.

She hadn't had much private conversation with him since the campers had come. He usually spent the evenings with the social workers discussing the plans for the next day's activities, and by the time he returned to the house Gina was in bed fast asleep. Not once had she been kept awake at night by thoughts of Oliver and what might have been if he had not been killed. Nor did she think of him much during the daytime. She was too busy.

The youngsters attending the camp were a lively bunch, and all were grateful for their opportunity to enjoy the beautiful scenery and to participate in recreations which might otherwise have been denied to them. When it came to showing them how to sail, Will enlisted Gina's help and she gave dry land instruction on the simplest points of sailing before showing them how to rig the dinghies and launch them.

She enjoyed seeing the bright red sails of the small boats fluttering against the blues and greens of the loch on a fine day and often wished she had time to go sailing herself. Hearing Will enter the kitchen behind her, she voiced her wish aloud to him.

'There'll be plenty of time when they've gone,' he said, then to her surprise he brushed her cheek with the back of his hand in that strangely affectionate gesture he had used once before. This time she didn't flinch away from him.

'You're looking better,' he remarked. 'Behaving better, too. Not so your cat, though. Look at this!'

He held out his arm and pushed back his shirt sleeve to reveal a long deep scratch on the inside of his wrist.

'Oh, how did you get that?' exclaimed Gina.

'Rescuing your foolish animal.'

'When? Where? You didn't tell me.'

'I'm telling you now, aren't I?' he retorted. 'He seems to be fascinated by high places. The more dangerous they are the better. He had somehow scrambled down the cliffs at the end of the loch and he was stuck on a ledge, and letting out the most ear-splitting cries. I climbed down and managed to grab him. The scratch was my reward for effort.'

'Thank you,' said Gina, faintly. She had a sudden vision of the cliffs, dark and forbidding, as she had often seen them, rearing up against the backcloth of the sunset. At the foot of them the sea flung itself against tumbled rocks. If Blue had fallen he would have been dashed to pieces against those rocks. If Will had slipped he would have gone too, his body hurtling over and over through the air into the heaving smashing water.

Her mouth trembled suddenly. Tears brimmed in her eyes. He had said she looked better, but she was still easily upset by the thought of death.

'Are the tears for me or for the cat?' he asked derisively.

She blinked furiously and glared at him.

'For both of you. You could have been killed.'

'Not I. I'm too experienced a climber to take any unnecessary risks. If I'd thought there was a chance of me slipping I'd have come back for a rope. But you'll have to watch him. He likes this place and he's beginning to run wild. There's nothing to stop him from straying on to the Macneal estate and if Grant Parker, the game warden, sees him he might shoot first and ask questions afterwards.'

'Oh, surely he wouldn't shoot a kitten?'

'Oh, yes, he would. Those grouse moors are the Macneal pride and joy and Parker raises some of the finest game in the country. He won't take kindly to a stray cat amongst his special pigeons. So keep your precious Blue near you, if you can.'

'I'll try, but I've been so busy, and it isn't always possible to keep him in with the door forever opening.'

'I know. That's why I didn't want you to bring him. And don't think I haven't noticed how hard you've been working. You're not feeling so sorry for yourself now, are you?'

'No, I'm not,' she admitted. 'I must have been a pain in the neck after Oliver was killed,' she added, unconsciously using one of his own phrases to describe her miserable behaviour.

'You were,' he agreed. 'And your mother was at her wits' end wondering what to do about you. Are you glad you came here to try Fox's remedy for all ills?'

'Now that isn't a good question to ask at the moment. Ask me when my back isn't aching and my hands are restored to their normal state,' she riposted.

He laughed and, putting his arm round her shoulders, hugged her gently.

'Mrs Chadwick was wrong. You have plenty of spunk, and anyone who says otherwise will have me to reckon with,' he said softly.

Surprised by the hug, and more than a little perturbed by the effect being close to him was having on her, she sought refuge in flippancy.

'Kitten-soft, you called me,' she accused.

'And so you are,' he murmured. His hand slipped down

90

over her shoulder and slid under her arm.

She looked up to object. He bent his head swiftly and kissed her on the mouth. Gina sprang away from him, startled and quivering.

'How dare you!' she exclaimed, unable to think of anything else to say, knowing she sounded ridiculously prudish.

'I dared because I wanted to kiss you to thank you for all you've done recently. You won't let me pay you because you volunteered to come, so I have to find another way of expressing my appreciation,' he explained coolly. 'Now come off it, George, stop behaving as if I'm the villain in some Victorian melodrama. What's a kiss between friends?'

He was laughing at her, and she could not bear his laughter any more than she could bear his kiss, no matter how lightly it had been given. Turning, she fled up the stairs, every nerve tingling. Blue chased up after her, as usual, but for once she had forgotten him and, inadvertently, she shut him out of the room in her desire to be alone with her tumultuous thoughts. His scratching and mewling took her back to the door again. She opened it impatiently and let him in.

'It was all your fault, you silly kitten,' she muttered. Ignoring her, Blue strolled across to the mat on which he slept every night, stretched out full length on his side and blinked drowsily at her.

'If you hadn't been on that ledge,' Gina continued, 'he wouldn't have had to rescue you. Then you wouldn't have scratched him and he wouldn't have told me about the scratch. Then I wouldn't have said what I did and he wouldn't have been tempted to do what he did.'

It all made sense to Gina, but Blue didn't think much of the explanation and yawned disgustedly before licking his forepaw and passing it over one ear.

Still quivering, Gina undressed and quickly climbed into the cold bed. The effect of Will's kiss on her was alarming. Viewing it now from the shelter of her room, she knew that he had given it as he had said, in friendliness, as a way of

91

showing his appreciation. Her violent over-reaction had been quite uncalled for.

It would have been different, she agreed with herself, if they hadn't been alone in the house. It would have been different if she hadn't been all keyed up to marry Oliver only to have her desires frustrated by his sudden death. It would have been different if Will hadn't married a girl called Bridget, who might turn up any day because the swans were back in the glen, a sure sign that the true mistress of the master of the glen would return soon.

Gina groaned, tired of the tug-of-war of argument, and fell asleep surprisingly quickly and slept as soundly as she had always slept in that bed.

To her relief Will made no reference to her odd behaviour when she met him briefly before serving breakfast the next morning, and during the next few days there were no more conversations alone with him before bedtime.

Storms blew in from the Atlantic and the water in the loch was churned up under the onslaught of wild wind and sleety rain. Two of the campers out on their four-day camp returned sodden and miserable, their tent having been washed away by a rushing torrent of water which had suddenly developed on the mountainside where they had been spending the night. Another lost his way on the moors and a search party had to be organised to find him when he didn't turn up. He was found and brought back triumphantly by the boys whom Will had taken with him on the search and who had all apparently enjoyed climbing perpendicular rock for the first time in their lives.

Will took all the crises in his stride, turning each 'adventure' into an object lesson for the entire group. His calmness and foresight were remarkable, thought Gina. He was always able to think his way out of a difficult situation, but he never took unnecessary risks. He handled the young people easily and with humour, but when they had all gone he admitted that he had missed Gavin, and that it was important that he found someone suitable to take Gavin's place before the next group arrived in May because they would have no social workers with them, but would be private individuals paying for the chance to participate in some 'adventures'.

It was with that in mind that he left her and Lachie in charge of the farm and drove down to Glasgow to look up an old Army acquaintance. Feeling rather pleased that he trusted her sufficiently to stay and look after his home, Gina took the opportunity to relax and explore the glen.

The weather had changed again and was mild and sunny. There were many more signs of spring than had been visible when she had arrived. The icing was still on the summit of Ben Searg, but it had shrunk and in the woodland, which covered the lower slopes of the mountain, there was a glow of pink as buds swelled.

Gina fed the swans every day. They were becoming more used to her and no longer reached out their necks in ugly attack. They did not like Blue, however, and the frisky kitten was sensible enough to keep a safe distance from those snapping beaks and muscular necks.

One day when feeding time was over Gina wandered along the edge of the loch, intending to go as far as the opposite shore which had always attracted her. As usual Blue accompanied her, occasionally disappearing into the undergrowth of brambles and reappearing ahead of her.

After one disappearance he did not come back. Having found that the distance to the opposite side of the loch was much further than she had anticipated, Gina wished to return to White Lodge. The absence of the kitten, however, made her unwilling to return without him as she remembered Will's warning about the possibility of the kitten being shot by the game warden of the Macneal estate.

Calling to Blue, she walked on a little further until she came to some wire fencing. It didn't look like electric fencing, so she ducked through the strands and went on, still calling to the cat.

After a while she decided it was silly to walk any further,

so she sat down on a convenient boulder of rock and awaited Blue's reappearance. As Lachie would say, there was really no need for her to hurry. She might as well relax and enjoy the view. From her position she could see another aspect of the dark tower and behind it, winking through the screen of birches, the white walls of the house.

The afternoon was still and quiet. No cry of seagull or whaup disturbed the peace. Even the water was silent.

'I suppose you realise you're trespassing?'

The voice was masculine and rather husky. She turned to find a young man of her own age standing a few feet away from her. He was tall and too thin. His handsome face was a pale wedge framed by a tangle of longish black hair. His eyes were as dark as his hair, opaque and unwinking. He was dressed in well-cut tweed pants and a beautiful cream-coloured Aran sweater. Between his hands was Blue.

'Is this yours,' asked the young man, not waiting for her to answer his first question.

'Yes. Where did you find him?'

'Stalking a pair of robins who are busy building their nest. You'd best take him. If Parker sees him he'll shoot him.'

He spoke gently and his smile was diffident yet disarming. Gina took Blue from him and thanked him.

'I wouldn't have trespassed if I hadn't lost him,' she explained apologetically.

'I couldn't care less whether you trespass or not,' he replied. 'You're from the White Lodge, aren't you?'

'Yes.' Gina pushed some tendrils of hair back from her face and the sunlight caught in the diamond on her finger, making it flash. 'I'll go back now that I have him,' she added.

'Do you mind if I walk with you? I've nothing else to do. Mother sent me out to get some air, but there's nothing more dull than walking by myself. Before the storms started I used to come down to the beach here and watch you through the binoculars.'

'Oh.' She was dismayed. He grinned rather sheepishly. 'Do you mind?'

'Yes, I do. Why didn't you come over and make yourself known to us instead of spying?'

'I wasn't really spying. It was just something to do. I suppose I should have come over. Andrea keeps saying I should meet Will Fox, and Mother thinks an adventure course would be good for me. Make a man of me, she says.' He laughed rather mirthlessly. 'But I'm a man already and I don't want to be done good to. I've been ill.'

She could see that he had. His face had the pallor of someone who had recently spent a long time in hospital.

'What was wrong?' she asked gently, feeling a surge of sympathy towards him.

'Car accident,' he said gruffly, as if it hurt him to talk about it. 'Multiple fractures, then pneumonia. Oh, don't be too sympathetic. It was my own fault. I was driving too fast on a wet greasy road and the car skidded. I always drive too fast,' he added in a low, defiant voice.

He was really desperately unhappy, thought Gina, in need of help in the same way she had been after Oliver had been killed.

'Was there anyone else in the car at the time of the crash?' she asked, thinking it might help him to talk to a complete stranger about it.

'Yes. That's why I didn't want to go on living afterwards,' he mumbled.

Exactly as she had felt. Then Will had appeared on the scene and had forced her back into life.

'A girl?' she persisted.

'Yes.' He closed his eyes tightly as if to prevent her from seeing tears brim in them. 'My girl-friend. We'd just decided to split, or at least she'd decided. She knew my mother didn't approve of her. Now she's in intensive care and may not live.'

'Who is Mother?' asked Gina, deciding to ignore the break in his voice.

'I thought you'd know,' he exclaimed.

'I've only been at White Lodge for just over two weeks, and I've been so busy that I haven't had time to find out about neighbours.'

He was staring at her curiously.

'Then you must have come with the swans,' he said.

'Yes, I did.'

'How odd, but it fits in with the legend, doesn't it?' he exclaimed.

Gina was startled. She couldn't see how her coming to the glen fitted the legend at all.

'Does it? I don't see how.'

'Oh, never mind. Forget it. I'm Gregor Macneal,' he said as they moved side by side back along the shore. 'My mother is the chief of the clan and you've been trespassing on her estate.'

'Will it be yours one day?'

He shook his head with a glimmer of a smile.

'No. My eldest brother is the heir. I'm just the no-good youngest son,' he replied. 'It'll be his when she dies, and that won't be for years and years. Like Victoria Regina, she'll outlive everyone. She's a tough nut, and the only person I've heard of who doesn't seem to be afraid of her is Will Fox. As a result she has it in for him.'

'Why?'

'Because he goes his own way without consulting her, but mostly I suppose because he owns the glen and she would like to see it as part of the Macneal estate again. She was furious when she learned that the Hendersons had sold it behind her back. She tried to buy it back off Will, but he wouldn't sell. Then he started the adventure camps. She'd love to find out some black mark against him so that she could hold it over him and make him dance to her tunes, but she can't. His Army career was without blemish. His dealings with the local authorities are above board, and as far as anyone can tell his morals are of good repute. So she's been trying something else.'

'What is that?'

'My young sister, Andrea, has taken a liking to him, so Mother is encouraging her. She thinks that as her son-in-law Will Fox might be more amenable to her ideas.'

'Oh, but——' began Gina, and then stopped short. She had been about to say that Will was already married, then she had realised that that piece of information was not hers to pass on, and that Will would be annoyed if he learned she had been talking about his personal life, especially since he did not do that himself. It was quite obvious that the Macneal family knew no more about Bridget than Lachie did.

'But of course when Mother sees you she'll realise that he's scotched that move on her part too.'

'Sees me?' Gina was absolutely mystified.

'Yes,' said Gregor with a grin which seemed to gloat over the possibility of his mother being discomfited. 'She's not going to like you one little bit. I'm going to leave you here because it's quite a long walk back to the castle and I'm not up to walking a long way yet. Thanks for letting me talk to you.'

There was light in his dark eyes now, a gleam of admiration as they roved over her smoothly coiled red-glinting brown hair and creamy-skinned heart-shaped face.

'Please come and see us at the Lodge whenever you feel like a change. There won't be any more campers for another month,' said Gina impulsively.

'I'd like to come,' he said simply. 'But perhaps I should warn you, now I've found someone like you in this wilderness where nothing ever happens I'm likely to make a nuisance of myself. You haven't told me your name.'

'It's Gina.'

'Gina, the nut-brown maiden, who came with the swans,' he murmured, and his smile appeared, not so diffident this time, but infinitely charming. 'Yes,' he added, 'the glen is going to be quite different now that you're here.'

The meeting with Gregor Macneal made Gina feel light hearted. It was nice to know that there was someone about her own age living near with whom she had something in common, even if it was only a fatal car accident. She thought about him several times during the next two days while she was busy about the house. He was handsome and cultured, yet had a touch of wildness which was attractive. She was looking forward to seeing him again when he came on his promised visit to the Lodge.

Sunlight and soft winds made cleaning a must. Gina swept away winter cobwebs and washed everything that was washable. She had never had this urge to make everything clean before, but then she had never had a house to herself before. And if she didn't spring-clean White Lodge, who would?

In a frenzy of energy she washed blankets and curtains and strung them on the line in the garden to blow in the gentle breezes. Later she beat the dust out of rugs and mats. In the house she washed paintwork and floors.

Astonished by her burst of activity, Lachie, who was taking his time to plough Will's fields ready for sowing grain, shook his head at her and told her that if she wasn't careful she'd be getting indigestion. She laughed at him and told him she didn't care. The house was going to be clean and sparkling before Will returned.

'He won't notice,' muttered Lachie, in pessimistic mood.

'Think not?' challenged Gina. 'Want to bet?' He looked surprised.

'Ach, now, and me not a betting man,' he moaned, shifting his pipe from one side of his mouth to the other.

'I'll tell you what we'll do, then,' said Gina. 'You know that lovely old pewter jug you have sitting on the mantelpiece in your cottage?'

'I do that. It was my grandmother's and her mother's before her. Family heirloom, that's what it is.'

'Then will you lend it to me?'

'Now why should I being doing that?'

'I want to arrange some flowers in it.'

'And where will you be after getting the flowers?'

'You're going to show me where the primroses grow,' replied Gina.

'Primroses? That's easy.'

'Not today—tomorrow morning. I'm going to arrange them in the jug and I'm going to put it on the kitchen table. If Will notices them and the clean house I keep the jug. If he doesn't you can have it back. Do you agree?'

Lachie's eyes twinkled as he looked down at her.

'Ach, it's a winning way you have with you lass, for all you're a sassenach. I agree.'

By evening that day Gina was tired with her efforts at house-cleaning, but there was one last job to do, and that was to tidy the big roll-topped desk in the living room where Will kept all the correspondence pertaining to the camps. She had been wanting to tidy it ever since she had started to help him to answer the applications.

It took quite a long time because she discovered, to her dismay, that Will's private correspondence was mixed up with the business stuff. There were letters from his mother, letters from Meg Maxwell, postcards from friends on holiday in various parts of the world. Gina decided that she must suggest to Will that if he was going to continue with the adventure camps he should obtain a proper filing system.

Then she brought her thoughts to a full stop.

'Stop it, Gina,' she said. 'You're only a volunteer. Don't get too involved because one day you'll be leaving.'

She threw away the clutter of unwanted paper and then began to sort the remainder into neat piles. While doing so she came across the invitation to her own wedding. The sight of it brought tears to her eyes and held up the job of tidying for a few minutes.

When she began again she came across several letters written on pink perfumed paper. The postmark on the envelope was German. Her curiosity getting the better of her, thinking they might be letters once written to Will by Bridget, Gina took the sheet of paper out of one envelope. To her surprise the letter was written in a language she recognised as being German. It was signed with the name Irma.

She was glad she didn't understand the language because she was sure she would have been tempted to read the letter if it had been written in English. As it was she felt slightly embarrassed, as if she had stumbled upon a secret in Will's life, and she pushed the pink envelopes away in a pigeon-hole, and spent the rest of her hours awake, wondering who Irma was and why she should write so many letters to Will.

CHAPTER FOUR

NEXT morning Lachie showed Gina where the primroses were hiding in warm secret places near a burn where it rushed down to the loch. Delighted to find the pale yellow flowers protected by their oblong leaves, the surfaces of which were wrinkled and furry, Gina picked as many as she could with fairly long stems, and took them back to the house. There she arranged them in the pewter jug which she discovered had been designed in the reign of George the Second and had the lovely curves and decorated handle of that period.

There were no tablecloths in the house big enough to cover the long table, but she had found a length of the cotton cretonne which someone, she guessed it was Madge Anderson, had used to make curtains. Placed cornerwise on the table it added colour and brightness to the room. In the middle she set the jug of primroses and birch catkins, which she had also collected, and stood back to admire the effect.

'I mind my wife used to do the same,' said Lachie with a sigh.

'And didn't you like her doing it?' asked Gina, interested.

'Aye, I did, but I never said so to her.'

'Oh? Why not?'

'Ach, she would have had flowers all over the house, even in the privy, and what use are flowers to a man when all he's wanting is good food after a hard day in the fields? And when I'd be reminding her of that she'd look at me and she'd quote the Bible at me. "Man shall not live by bread alone," she'd say. She was very knowledgeable about the Bible. She was a Sunday school teacher at the kirk.'

'She was right too. There are more important things in life than eating all the time.'

'Aye, but not when you're hungry, lass.'

'Where is Mrs Munro now?' asked Gina. Lachie would never let her have the last word on principle and could be as exasperating as any other man when he wanted to be.

'Under the green sod in Lochinvie kirkyard, God rest her soul,' he intoned with mournful reverence.

'But I thought you said she left the glen because it couldn't hold a woman?'

'So she did leave, in a box made of elm wood. Beautiful, it was,' murmured Lachie, his blue eyes smoky as he looked into the past.

'When was that?'

'Let me see now. Kirsty is almost thirty—aye, it must be thirty-one years ago. She was lovely, so she was, but the bairn was too strong for her, whatever.'

'Bairn? You mean she died in childbirth?'

'That was the way of it. We couldn't get her to the hospital in time. My sister took on the rearing of Kirsty. It wouldn't have done to let her stay in the glen. Now she's married to Kenny Ross, a fisherman in Ullapool, and has bairns of her own. She serves in the chandler's shop. You'll be going there and having a wee talk with her one day.'

He drifted out of the kitchen into the warm sunshine of late April and Gina watched him go, feeling bemused, as she always did after a conversation with Lachie. He was so contented with his lot here, living alone in the glen, and it was difficult to imagine him as a young man. Even more difficult was it to imagine him as a father and grandfather. The similarity of his story to that of the chief of the glen whose wife had disappeared and also to that of Will, whose wife had left him, worried her a little. She wouldn't like Will to become like Lachie, she thought.

She was in her room sewing the zipper which had worked loose on her jeans when she heard the sound of a vehicle coming down the road. Flinging the jeans aside, she went across to the window. It was the blue truck, dusty after its journey. To her surprise close behind it came a shiny black car—a Rolls-Royce.

If the black car had not been there she would have rushed down the stairs to fling open the door to welcome Will home, but instead she lingered in her room to finish the sewing.

Once it was finished she could contain herself no longer. She had to find out who had come in the car, and to find out if Will had noticed the primroses. Changing into the smooth wheat-coloured pants and fluffy sweater she had worn the first day she had met Will, she swathed her hair into its chignon. Thinking how much her complexion had improved with the use of the soft water of the glen, she applied a touch of make-up to eyes and mouth, and then, with a sudden urge to look her best, she hung golden hoop ear-rings in her ears.

Half way down the narrow stairs she paused on hearing a woman's voice, clear and autocratic.

'So when Gregor came with a tale that he'd met the young woman who was staying here, when he was out walking, I just had to come and see her for myself.'

Gina froze where she stood and waited for Will's reply.

'And see her you shall.'

There was a lilt of laughter in his voice, which put her on guard at once. Will Fox was up to mischief.

He came out of the living room into the hall, and the sight of his waving blue-black hair above the breadth of his tweed-clad shoulders made her feel suddenly weak and she caught hold of the banister to support herself. She had not reckoned on being glad to see him.

His foot on the bottom stair he raised his head and saw her.

'Oh, there you are. I was wondering what had happened to you,' he said, his glance taking in her pink-tinged face and the soft curves of her figure outlined by the clinging knit pants and sweater. 'My word, you are dressed up. Expecting company?' he asked cheekily.

Oh, he was on form all right. Unholy glee seemed to be

dancing in his light blue eyes and all her pleasure at seeing him was pushed aside by irritation with his mischievous mood.

'No. I dress to please myself,' she retorted.

Creases appeared in his cheeks as he grinned.

'The get-up isn't wasted,' he drawled. 'We have company. The local gentry, all three of them. They've come to size you up, and also to find out if you and I are living in sin, so watch how you go.'

Warning was implicit in his words and he closed one eye in an outrageous wink. Immediately she was reminded of the act he and Birdie had put on the night of the party at the flat.

He swung away down the stairs again. Apprehensively she followed him. As she reached his side he placed a possessive arm about her shoulders and urged her into the room.

'Here she is, Mrs Macneal. Georgina Marriott, my fiancée,' he announced.

Gina was aware of several things at once; the sudden tension in the room as Will swept her into it; the painful grip of his hand on her elbow as he held it after her attempt to slip out of his casual hold on her shoulder; the violent emotional upheaval his announcement caused within her, which made her turn her head to glare up at him.

His eyes laughed down into hers and with just the faintest sardonic twist to the corner of his mouth he murmured,

'This is Mrs Elena Macneal of Castle Duich, sweetheart, chief of the Macneal clan, her youngest son Gregor, whom I think you've already met, and her daughter Andrea.'

Sweetheart, indeed! Anger sizzled within Gina. She would get her own back on him for his presumptuousness somehow, she vowed.

Across the room she saw Gregor leaning against the wall behind one of the armchairs. He smiled at her and nodded. In the armchair was a tall slim girl of about eighteen years of age. She had a mop of black hair, a dark-browed sulky face, and was dressed in stained jodhpurs, muddy riding boots and a high-necked white sweater.

'Never mind them. I'm the one who has come to see you,' the autocratic voice which had spoken before belonged to the small woman in her late fifties who sat perched on the edge of another armchair. She was wearing a magnificent kilt with a white blouse and a jacket of dark tweed. Her face was modelled on austere lines and wore an expression of imperiousness. The only resemblance to her two youngest children lay in her fine dark brown eyes. Her hair was grey and was cut short.

Her training in good manners asserting itself, Gina moved forward with her hand stretched out.

'I'm very pleased to meet you, Mrs Macneal,' she said.

Her hand was taken and shaken and the dark brown eyes looked her over.

'I can't say the same,' retorted Elena Macneal, 'because it would be untrue. But you're better than I expected, much better. Where do you come from? I don't think I know anyone called Marriott. Sounds English to me.'

'From Warwickshire. My father is the managing director of a machine tool company. You may have heard of it—Marriott and Edwards,' returned Gina, her back up and the light of battle in her eyes as she recognised an attempt to discomfit her.

She had the pleasure of seeing the dark brown eyes widen, before they looked past her at Will.

'You've done well for yourself, Will Fox, perhaps not as well as you could have done if I'd had my way,' said Elena Macneal. 'How long have you been engaged?'

The question was shot at Gina and almost caught her off balance. She turned appealingly to Will.

'Sorry, darling,' she said softly. 'I can't remember how long. Does it really matter?'

He came forward and slipped an arm round her waist.

'I can't remember either,' he murmured, gazing down at her. 'About two or three weeks, I think.' He gazed at the all-observant chieftain of the clan Macneal. 'When one is blissfully happy one tends to lose count of time,' he added.

Gina had the greatest difficulty in controlling her laughter. Will was the last person she would expect to use such sentimental language. But it seemed to go down surprisingly well with Mrs Macneal. Her face softened and a faint smile appeared.

'I'm glad to hear someone is happy these days. So many young people seem to want to flout convention and not go in for engagements, or even marriage.' She sent a fierce glance in the direction of Gregor, who turned away and went to look out of the window. 'When are you thinking of getting married?' she asked Will.

'In the autumn, some time. We haven't set a date yet.'

'Very sensible,' replied Elena with a nod. 'You're going up in my estimation, Will Fox. It isn't good to rush into marriage. You need time to get to know one another.'

'That's why Gina came back north with me to stay for a while,' Will said suavely. 'You may have heard that the Andersons have gone, leaving me in rather a difficult position. Fortunately Gina is trained in institutional management and has been able to help out with the camp.'

Gregor moved restlessly and looked round at his brother.

'Now you've found out what you wanted to know don't you think we should leave?' he suggested. 'After all, Captain Fox has only just returned home and he and Miss Marriott must have a lot to talk about.'

Mrs Macneal sent a scathing glance in his direction.

'I'll leave when I'm ready and not when you tell me. Go and wait outside if you don't like the conversation,' she barked.

A dark mutinous expression crossed Gregor's face and for a moment it looked as if he might retaliate. Then he turned and walked swiftly out of the room and out of the house.

'Please excuse Gregor's lack of manners,' said Mrs Macneal. 'He's been very ill, poor boy. We thought we'd lost

106

him. And now he doesn't seem to want to face up to life at all. I was wondering whether you could do anything to help him, Will. He did some climbing and sailing when he was at school. In fact he was very keen on outdoor activities when he was younger. I thought that perhaps he could help you run one of your camps. It would get him out of doors and give him something to think about other than himself and that ... that young woman.'

'No,' replied Will firmly, his eyes glinting like steel. There was no mischief in him now. Nothing of the fond lover either, thought Gina.

Mrs Macneal drew herself even more upright. Her eyes flashed and her bosom heaved, in reaction to his insolence, and Gina decided it was time she took a hand in the proceedings.

'Surely this can be discussed sensibly before any decision is made,' she said softly. 'I'll make some tea. I spent the morning baking and I'm longing to try out my chocolate cake on someone. Please won't you stay and have some?'

She turned to Andrea Macneal, who until now had been silent and sulky, but the young woman deliberately ignored her, an expression of boredom on her patrician features.

'Afternoon tea has always been one of my weaknesses,' said Mrs Macneal, suddenly gracious. 'You've been well trained, lass, by your mother. Take note, Andrea.'

Gina turned to Will.

'Will darling,' she purred, giving him one of her up-from-under looks, 'please make Mrs Macneal feel at home while I go and make the tea.'

He gave her in return one of his dagger-bright glances, which told her more than anything else that he didn't take kindly to being told what to do by her. She had more than got her own back for being called sweetheart by him.

Gina was just filling the kettle when she was surprised by the appearance of Andrea, who strolled into the kitchen her hands in the pockets of her jodhpurs. Now that the young woman was standing up Gina could see that her figure was flat and boyish and that there was a certain awkwardness in her manner. Andrea was really not much more than a schoolgirl.

'It's strange that Will has never mentioned you to us,' said Andrea, leaning against the table and watching Gina's busy hands as she set crockery on a tray. The girl's voice was deep like her mother's and had the same slight suggestion of Highland sibilance in it.

Gina looked up and smiled brightly as she recognised an attempt to put her on the spot.

'He's never mentioned you to me either,' she replied coolly. 'But then he isn't a very communicative man. Possibly he forgot all about you when he was staying in the south with us.'

Andrea scowled, an expression which did nothing to help her face, bringing, as it did, her thick dark eyebrows together across the top of her bold prominent nose. The edge of her straight white teeth explored her full lower lip. Obviously she didn't like being blocked in her attempt to disconcert Will's suspiciously new fiancée.

'You're not at all the sort of person I'd have expected him to want to marry,' she persisted.

'What sort of person did you expect?' asked Gina.

'Someone used to the outdoors, who would enjoy the activities he enjoys, who would know about farming and like living close to nature. You're so obviously more used to the city, and you look too soft and cuddlesome, like a pet,' replied Andrea, with a sneer.

A cup rattled in its saucer as Gina set it down. Careful, she warned herself. She must not let this abrupt sulky girl upset her.

'But then it's well known that men and women often choose their opposites as their partners for life,' she said gently. It was surprising how useful her own mother's comments on life could be. She had never thought she would be passing them off as her own philosophy.

'I think that to have interests in common is much more

108

important if a relationship is to be successful and survive,' said Andrea sharply, anger burning in her dark eyes. 'You know nothing about farming or about living here.'

'I can learn,' replied Gina quietly, noting the unhappiness in Andrea's face. It seemed that the chief of the clan Macneal had more than one unhappy ill-adjusted child!

There was no doubt that Andrea was very upset. She was not only suspicious of Will's engagement, she was hurt by it because, encouraged by her mother, she had probably come to regard him as her property.

'What will you do here when winter comes and the road is washed away?' demanded Andrea agitatedly. 'How will you manage with no entertainment, no shops, with Lachie as your only neighbour? Madge Anderson wasn't able to put up with life in the glen, and she had lived in the Highlands before, so how do you think you will manage?'

The deep voice was thick with scorn. Gina stared helplessly as understanding of this new complication hit her.

'I'm sorry you've been disappointed. I wish I could help you,' she said impulsively and rather foolishly.

Andrea, whose wits were quick, noted the foolishness and pounced on it immediately.

'Help?' she exclaimed harshly. 'How can you help me? The only way you could do that would be to return your engagement ring to Will and to go away from here and never come back.'

Her voice choked suddenly, she whirled on her heels and ran from the room. Staring down at Oliver's ring, Gina heard voices in the hall, then the front door closed noisily and the house was ominously silent.

'Make that tea for two only, you and me,' said Will drily as he came into the kitchen. 'Mrs Macneal has left too.'

'Oh, you were rude to her again,' exclaimed Gina as she poured water into the tea-pot.

His grin was unrepentant as he leaned against the table and helped himself to chocolate cake.

'Not rude, just honest. I told her I didn't want her playboy no-good son helping me, least of all if she's going to push him at me. I've had enough of her pushing Andrea at me. By the way, the daughter looked as if the world had come to an end as she went out of the house. What did you say to her? Were you rude? Or just honest, like me?'

'You should know why she was upset,' retorted Gina. 'She's in love with you, and she can't bear the thought of you being engaged to me.'

He let out a crack of scornful laughter.

'Love? Is that what you call it? More like a schoolgirl crush just because I've noticed her and have talked to her a few times.' His mouth twisted bitterly. 'I've had enough of that sort of love in the past and I can do without it now. It has a way of fading fast when faced with the reality of living with the object of worship.'

Gina looked at him sharply, but he didn't elaborate and went on eating his cake. When he had finished it he said,

'Now it's time you explained why you told Gregor we're engaged.'

'I didn't,' she replied indignantly. 'When I met him on the shore he did most of the talking.'

'Then where did he get the idea?'

Gina pushed a cup of tea across the table to him and as she did so noticed Oliver's diamond flashing on her finger.

'He must have noticed my ring and drawn his own conclusions,' she said in a stifled voice. 'Oh, what a mess! *You* could have denied it,' she rebuked him.

He stood up and came across to her, lifted her left hand and examined the ring.

'Yes, I suppose it was the ring that convinced him,' he murmured, ignoring her rebuke. 'Strangely enough I'd thought of suggesting to you that you stop wearing it or put it on your other hand. Diamonds—a girl's best friend. Did you choose them?'

'Oliver and I agreed that they were the most suitable,' she replied faintly, wondering why she felt peculiar whenever he came close to her.

'Oh, eminently suitable,' he commented ironically. 'As well as being a good investment. I've no doubt, either, that that was how Noll regarded *you*. A good investment.' He looked up and met her wide hurt gaze, and said softly, 'Now, if I were really engaged to you I'd give you topazes to match your eyes.'

Perturbed by the remark as well as by the expression in his eyes, she snatched her hand away, picked up the tea pot and began to pour tea for herself.

'But you're not engaged to me,' she retorted shakily. 'May I know why you didn't deny it?'

He gave her one of his bright stabbing glances, finished drinking his tea and said with uncharacteristic evasiveness,

'I'll tell you later. Just now I have work to do and I've no more time for chit-chat. Lachie's fallen behind with the ploughing.'

He went from the room and she heard him dash up the stairs, presumably to change into working clothes. She stared at the primroses and felt the first stirrings of disappointment. He hadn't noticed them after all.

Will was busy out of doors until twilight and Gina could hear the monotonous sound of the tractor which pulled the plough as it crossed and re-crossed one of the fields. When he came in he brought Lachie with him to share the evening meal Gina had prepared, and she sat silent all through the meal listening to Lachie's voice droning on about this and that, hoping he would go when he had finished eating so that she could confront Will about the question of their 'engagement'.

But Lachie was in no hurry to leave, and Will, in a relaxed and easygoing mood now that he was back in his home, encouraged him to stay and play cribbage. They invited Gina to join them in a game, but she refused, pleading that she had some sewing to do.

Leaving them in the kitchen she went into the living room and tried to be interested in doing some petit-point embroidery. It was one of a set of seat covers for the dining room chairs which her mother had given her for a wedding present.

Sewing, however, made her restless. She found herself recalling Oliver's and her plans for their future together. It was the first time she had thought consciously about him since she had left Birmingham and she discovered she was now able to look at everything in a much more objective light. Her view was no longer obstructed by that terrible aching sense of loss.

Cut and dried. So her mother had called those plans, and had suggested that Oliver had not been in love with her. That afternoon Will, in a strangely mean and cynical mood, had said that Oliver had probably regarded her as a good investment. It was odd that he, Oliver's brother, and her mother should think alike about Oliver. Did that mean it was true, that Oliver had not loved her ecstatically and passionately, above all else, as she wanted to be loved, but had seen in her only a suitable wife for an ambitious doctor who would do all the right conventional things?

But then had she loved him ecstatically, and passionately, above all else, or had the great distress she had felt at the time of his death merely been the result of the blow her ego had suffered because she had not been married after all that big build-up?

Gina made a small sound of distress. She did not wish to think about it any more. Casting aside the petit-point, she wondered where Blue was. She hadn't seen her pet since just before supper.

She went into the kitchen. Lachie was still talking and she wondered, a little unkindly, if he ever stopped. Will, who was lounging indolently in his chair, looked rather somnolent, and she wondered if the whisky was affecting him. Certainly the level in the bottle on the table had gone down considerably since she had left them, but she knew that Lachie had an amazing tolerance for his native drink and could absorb large quantities of it without any visible effect.

She asked them if either of them had seen Blue. Will shook his head negatively without glancing up from his cards. Lachie, after a brief thought, said he hadn't either, but he was minded of a legend concerning cats and the island of Raasay a story into which he launched with fervour.

Irritated, Gina left the room abruptly and went upstairs. Blue wasn't in her room, so she took a jacket and scarf, went downstairs and let herself out of the house.

The evening air was soft and mild. A hazy moon peeped from behind a cloud so that finding her way down the path to the loch was made easy. Calling Blue occasionally, she walked slowly and thought about the two men playing cards in the house.

She was sure, now, that Will had brought Lachie in for a meal and had asked him to stay and play cards because he did not wish to be alone with her, and possibly because he still wanted to evade having to tell her why he hadn't denied they were engaged. But she was determined to have it out with him, and as soon as she had found Blue she would return to the house and think up some reason to get rid of Lachie.

Shingle crunched beneath her feet as she reached the shore. Wavelets were falling in moonlit frills in the narrow beach. To the north the sky was still streaked with light and she wondered if she would be in the glen long enough to see the northern lights.

It was such a remote place; a place of almost fairy-tale beauty, and there were times when she wondered whether she was really there or whether she was having a dream. Perhaps she was in one of those deep drug-induced slumbers which she had known after Oliver's death. Perhaps soon she would awake in the dark, sad and lonely, and would weep when she found that Glengorm did not exist and that Will Fox and all the other people she had met recently were but shadows, existing only in her imagination.

The crunch of footsteps on the shingle behind her was not dreamlike. Someone else was there with her. She turned

113

and saw him dark and bulky against the sheen of moonlit water.

'Are you there, George?'

She was tempted to play a game with him, to remain silent and creep off into the shadow of the birches and hide from him.

But even as she turned to do so he was beside her, more used to seeing in the dark than she was. His hand was on her arm, turning her to face him although she was sure he would not be able to see her face.

'What are you doing here?' he asked.

'Looking for Blue.'

'He came in just as Lachie was leaving,' he replied. 'I gave him some milk and the fish you'd cooked for him. I shut the door when I left the house so he can't get out again.'

'Thank you,' she said, and then sighed. 'I thought Lachie would never go.'

'Did you want him to?' He sounded surprised. 'And there was I thinking you'd be sorry for him because he's lonely. I thought you liked listening to his tales.'

'Not when I want to talk to you. You have something to explain,' she said shortly.

'I suppose you want to know if I had any success in finding someone to help with the May camp. The answer is no, I'm afraid, but Clarke Robertson has said he's willing to come for the summer.'

'Who is Clarke Robertson?' she asked with a touch of exasperation.

'The chap Andrew took me to see when we were down at Loch Lomond. He's a physical education teacher at a private school. His wife is willing to come and help too and they'll bring their two boys with them. It's probably better than having someone staying here permanently. I don't really need anyone here all winter.' He paused and added rather facetiously, 'Now that you and I are engaged I've no hesitation in asking you to stay on during May to help me with the next group of campers. When you go back south I can always say you changed your mind about marrying me and jilted me.'

Gina drew a slow breath and gritted her teeth. She supposed she should be grateful that he had brought up the subject of the engagement first, but his facetiousness found no echo in her.

'Will, it isn't like you to dodge an issue. Please tell me why you didn't deny what Gregor said,' she pleaded.

He didn't answer immediately. She could hear, the sound of the torrent falling over the rocks high up in the glen, and behind that sound was the muffled thunder of the sea breaking at the foot of the cliffs at the entrance to the loch.

'I thought I was backing you up,' he said eventually. 'I thought you'd told him we were engaged to protect yourself. Then I decided it was as good a way as any to protect my own good name as well as yours. It also created a suitable barrier between me and Andrea, who was becoming a bit of an embarrassment before I went to England.'

'Why do you want to protect your reputation?' she asked, thinking that all he had to do to keep Andrea at bay was to say he was married already.

'Well, you see, Mrs Macneal, as head of the clan, tends to rule the roost hereabouts. She has a great deal of influence with the local people. She doesn't like me because I'm an "incomer" and because I've taken over some land which she regards as still being Macneal property. She would love to find a way of making my life here uncomfortable and would go to any lengths, even so far as besmirching my reputation. Once she heard that there was a young woman living here and that the Andersons had left she thought she had the advantage. Fortunately for us her own son jumped to the wrong conclusion and saved me the trouble of having to think up some story to cover up.'

'But supposing Bridget, your wife, turns up?' she asked, voicing the worry which bothered her most.

His fingers bit cruelly into her arm, which he was still

115

holding.

'Bridget will not be coming back,' he said harshly. There was a short tense silence. Gina waited, hoping he would explain why Bridget would not be coming back, but when he spoke his voice was quiet and he made no reference to Bridget.

'Now that Clarke and his wife have promised to come I won't need to hold you to your promise to stay in the summer, but I'd be glad if you'd consider staying until they come at the beginning of July. Of course, if you feel like it you can stay on after they've come. You're welcome to stay as long as you like, George, until you're fully recovered from Oliver's death. Is that clear?'

She nodded silently because she was having difficulty in controlling the quiver of her lips as tears spurted to her eyes. When he spoke kindly like that it was her undoing. She could see quite clearly why he had brought her here and she knew that his cure was working.

But he had not seen her nod and the pressure of his fingers increased again as he peered at her and asked,

'Well? Is it clear?'

'Yes, yes, it's clear, Will, very clear. Thank you for explaining and for being so kind.'

Fingers touched her cheek and explored upwards moving against her wet eyelashes.

'Tears again?' he jeered gently. 'Softly!'

After that it seemed quite natural to be in his arms and held closely, while she sobbed her heart out as pent-up emotion overflowed.

Eventually her sobs subsided and she searched frantically in her jacket pocket for a handkerchief, only to find she had none.

'I haven't one either,' he said with a chuckle. 'You'll have to use your knuckles. Are you all right now?'

'Yes, thank you,' she sniffed. 'I'm sorry I broke down. It was just that you ...'

'Don't bother to explain, I understand,' he broke in

sharply. 'It had to happen sooner or later. Let's go back to the house now and on the way you can tell me what you think is wrong with Gregor Macneal.'

He took one of her hands in his as they walked side by side. The moon's radiance was growing stronger, striking sparks of light from the ice cap of the mountain, lining the outline of solitary trees and bushes, silvering the barks of the birches.

'He told me he'd been in a car crash. His girl-friend was hurt and may not survive, and it's his fault. He needs help, in the same way that I needed help that morning you came to see me.'

'Well, well,' he drawled lightly, 'you're coming on. You've actually admitted you were in a bad way. So now you're sorry for Gregor, are you?' His voice rasped queerly on the question. 'Beware of sympathy, George. Too much of it has a way of killing.'

'You could help him,' she said.

'What makes you think that?'

'You helped me.'

'But you, my dear almost sister-in-law, were only sunk in grief and merely needed rousing from it. Gregor's problem goes deeper than that. He's never been much good. You were good material to work with. The spunk was already there. It had just been smothered by soft living.'

'Couldn't that be true of Gregor too?'

They had reached the house. He opened the door and let her go through first. In the lamplit hall she turned and was shocked to see that his face was pale and drawn. His mouth was set in a hard controlled line and his eyes were narrowed as if he were in pain.

'Will, what's the matter?' she asked impulsively, placing a hand on his arm.

'Nothing much.' He shook off her hand impatiently as if he didn't like her to touch him. 'Just a twinge from an old wound. Let's hope you're right about Gregor because I've a feeling we're going to see a lot of him. Now that he's met you, he'll be round here by the hour, like his sister used to be. But don't expect me to welcome him with open arms. The best therapy for him is a certain amount of humiliation until he starts wanting to be recognised as someone who can do something positive.'

He turned back and opened the front door again and added,

'I've just remembered I forgot to close the barn door. Good night, George.'

She was sure he hadn't left the barn door open. He just wanted to be out of the house, away from her curiosity. She went up the stairs with a vague feeling of regret because he kept her shut out from his personal feelings. It was all right for him to comfort and help her, but she must not be allowed to comfort him. She was convinced the wound to which he had referred was not a physical one. Something she had said out there in the lovely spring moonlight had touched a sensitive spot.

Had it been her reference to Bridget? Why was he so cagey about his missing wife? Why was he so sure she would not be coming back to him?

The questions circled around Gina's mind as she prepared for bed, and remained unanswered, as usual. It was not until she had switched off the light and lay waiting for sleep to come that she realised that she was still saddled with the ridiculous complication of being 'engaged' to the man who had almost become her brother-in-law.

Next day she paid her first visit to Ullapool. The main reason for going was to stock up on gas and food. Gina sat beside Will in the front of the truck and was able to see the scenery through which she had travelled the night she had come to Glengorm.

Now that the month of May was in, changes were everywhere. It seemed to her that an artistic magician was at work, touching up the landscape with new colours. The dark pine forests were suddenly streaked with fresh light

118

green as larches came into leaf. Birch catkins were like golden tassels, swinging in the breeze. A shower of rain danced across the scene. Sunlight followed it and at once mountains and moors sparkled joyously as raindrops reflected the light.

Ullapool was quite a big village. Situated at the end of a large sea-loch, it had been built mostly in the eighteenth century to the order of the British Fishery Society. Its name was Norse in origin and meant Ulla's Home. It was as tidily arranged as only a planned settlement could be, with rows of whitewashed terraced houses sparkling in the sunlight.

Will parked the truck behind the curved seawall and pointed to the quay where the fishing boats huddled together.

'That's where I worked the first summer I owned Glengorm,' he said. 'I loaded lorries with fish.'

'Why?' asked Gina, surprised.

'No money,' he answered with a grin. 'Buying the estate cleaned out my bank balance. I used the little my father had left me, plus my savings. It was while I was working here that I had the idea for the adventure club.'

He opened the door and jumped down into the street. Gina got out her side of the vehicle, thinking that he would never cease to surprise her.

They went straight to the chandlers for the gas and were greeted by Lachie's daughter Kirsty, a rosy-cheeked, plump woman with her father's blue eyes. Those eyes turned to Gina and sized her up.

'A wee birdie brought me a piece of news this morning, and I'm thinking this is the young woman it concerns,' said Kirsty, her eyes twinkling.

'Oh, and what was the news?' asked Will casually.

'That you and she are engaged to be married. Is it true?'

'Yes,' said Will, before Gina could think. 'And who told you?'

'Mistress Parker, the gamekeeper's wife from Castle

119

Duich. She heard from the chief herself. Ach now, Will, aren't you going to introduce me? I feel I know the lass well already because Feyther has talked to me about her.'

Will introduced Gina, and Kirsty's sincere congratulations were accepted easily by him, but less easily by Gina.

'Feyther was right then, and there I was thinking he was having one of his daydreams. He told me the swans were back and that the curse had been lifted from the glen because they had brought with them the true mistress of the master of the glen. Ach, it's wonderful, so it is, after all those years.'

'A coincidence, nothing more,' said Will drily.

'Now isn't that just like you to be unromantic,' said Kirsty, sending a sympathetic glance in Gina's direction. 'Coincidence, indeed! If it is, Will Fox, it's a well-planned one.'

It was the same everywhere they went that morning. In other shops, on the quay where Will paused to greet some of his fishing acquaintances, in the hotel where they had their lunch. Mrs Macneal had done her work well in telling Mrs Parker, for it seemed that everyone who knew Will knew that he was engaged to Gina and there was nothing Gina could do about it.

'What are we going to do?' she wailed, as soon as the waitress had served them with their roast lamb.

'Nothing,' replied Will calmly. 'The fuss will soon die down. When you go, they'll nod their heads at one another and say they never expected yon young Sassenach lassie to stay in the glen. By then Andrea will have got over her infatuation.'

'And how will you like that? You'll look as if you've been let down again,' hissed Gina, suddenly furious with him.

His eyes, cool and wary, met hers across the table.

'Since I'll know it isn't true it won't worry me,' he said evenly.

'Well, how do you think I'll like it, having everyone think I couldn't put up with life in the glen and so I jilted you?' she exclaimed.

'The alternative is to have everyone talking about you now and saying something else which isn't true.'

'And that is?'

'That you and I are living together as man and wife without being married,' he said coolly. 'Take it or leave it, George. Perhaps you'd prefer to back out now and go back to Birmingham.'

She was caught. She supposed she could have walked out on him and gone back home, but it would mean letting him down, and she had agreed to stay to help him with the next group of campers. She had boasted once that she wasn't the sort of person who let people down, and at the back of her mind was Meg Maxwell's warning that Will had been let down too often in his life.

'No, I'm not backing out,' she heard herself saying firmly. 'I said I'd stay for the next camp, and stay I shall.'

He looked up at her and grinned.

'I thought you'd say that,' he said with maddening complacency, so that she wanted to shake him. He went on to talk about the rest of the shopping they had to do and she had to assume that he considered the matter settled. She was staying as his fiancée in the eyes of the neighbours, until such time as she wished to leave.

There was so much she didn't know about him, she thought, so much he kept hidden. When she had first met him she had believed him to be a roistering ex-soldier used to making easy conquests where women were concerned. Now she knew that his marriage had failed for some reason and that its failure had hurt him so much he could not talk about it, even to Meg, to whom she guessed he was closer than he was to any of his other relatives.

After the trip to Ullapool life settled down to comfortable routine. At that time of the year there was a great deal to do on the farm and often Will asked Gina to help by taking on such simple jobs as feeding the hens. She even learned how to milk a cow, and when he brought her a little lamb to look after because its mother had died, she was delighted.

The attention she gave to the lamb tended to make Blue jealous and one day the kitten roamed too far away, with the result that Gregor Macneal used his discovery of the cat on the grouse moors to come and make his first visit. He found Gina in the garden, perched on some rather shaky stepladders, trying to fix the clothes line which had become detached from one of its posts. He offered to fix it for her and she came down the ladder thankfully and took Blue from him.

When he had done the small job she thanked him again.

'For that you deserve a reward. Come and have a cup of tea and some home-made scones, and tell me what you've been doing since we last met.'

'I've been doing precisely nothing,' he replied. 'I've been bored to distraction and boring everyone else around me.'

'Then why didn't you come over as I suggested?' she asked, going into the house through the back door.

'I didn't like to intrude.'

'Intrude?' she was surprised.

'On you and Will. You're an engaged couple, remember.'

'But that needn't stop you from coming if you want to.'

'You're sure?'

'Oh, Gregor! How often do I have to say it? I'm sure. You're welcome to come any time.'

He didn't look any better than he had the last time she had seen him. If anything his cheeks were hollower and his eyes were more sunken, but he followed her into the house and wandered about the kitchen after her while she made tea and set out cups and saucers. Before the afternoon was over she knew all about his affair with Audrey, the girl who had been hurt in the accident, his dislike of his mother and her overbearing ways and his rather dismal attempts to free himself from her dominance.

'Every time I think I've escaped from her something awful happens like that accident and I'm dragged back to her,' he complained. 'She smothers me,' he added, with a twisted grin at his own pun. 'I wished I'd never been born with a silver spoon in my mouth. I might have grown up with a sense of responsibility if I had. But everything has been too easy and now I've reached the point when I can't find any reason for living.'

Gina didn't make any comment. She just let him talk, and after that first afternoon visit he came, as Will had predicted he would, every day. Some days he walked over, some days he came in a sports car which he said really belonged to Andrea. His had been smashed up in the accident and he hadn't bothered to buy another. In fact he was doubtful as to whether he was entitled to drive any more.

Every time he came Gina endeavoured to have a job for him to do, which helped her. At first he was diffident about helping her because he was afraid of what Will might say, and in fact the times when Will was present at the time of Gregor's arrival, he often made a disparaging remark about the young man. Gregor took these remarks with a meekness which Gina found alarming, but one day he blew up after Will had left the house.

'The trouble is, I know he's right,' he seethed. 'I am good for nothing. But since I've met you and him I've wanted to be good for something. Gina, isn't there anything I can do to show him that I can be positive and do things, that I'm not just a playboy and a parasite? Do you think he'd let me help him run his next camp?'

'I don't think so. Not unless you can show him what you can do before the campers come,' replied Gina, thinking of Will's blatant refusal to Mrs Macneal when she had suggested Gregor might help him. 'Do you have any skills you could pass on to others?'

'Apart from crashing cars, you mean,' he said with another twisted smile. 'I've done some rock-climbing. I used to swim for my school. I've done some sailing.'

123

'Could you rig a dinghy and launch it?' asked Gina, her eyes lighting up.

'Of course I could.'

'Then come on,' she cried gaily. 'I've been longing to go sailing, but there's been no one to go with.'

'What about Will?' he asked.

'He's been too busy. There's a lot to do on the farm and he has only Lachie to help him. Come on, let's go and get one of the dinghies out of the storage shed now, and rig it.'

He followed her out into the sunny afternoon. There was a breeze, enough to make a ripple on the water, enough to test a person's skill in sailing without the sail being too strenuous.

'You and Will are a strange couple,' Gregor ventured to comment while they were sorting out the rigging of the mast prior to stepping it on the deck of the dinghy.

Gina cast a wary glance at him.

'Why do you say that?'

'You don't act as I would expect an engaged couple to act.'

'How do you expect an engaged couple to act?'

He grinned at her and she realised suddenly how attractive he was now that his face was filling out and his eyes had lost their hunted look.

'I'm probably off course,' he said, 'but I thought you'd be much more ... Help! I don't know how to put it ... much more loving, I suppose. I've never seen him touch you, except on the day we came with Mother, and I've never heard him call you anything but George. The same goes for you too.'

'You must remember you're not here all the time,' she said quietly, hoping she sounded convincing.

He gave her a sharp glance and then had the grace to blush.

'I see. No, I'm not. Sorry, Gina, I didn't mean to probe, I suppose you and Will are just as much in love with each other as the next engaged couple is. You wouldn't be here helping him if you weren't in love with him. I mean, it isn't the sort of place a woman like you wants to be buried in unless . . .' He was floundering badly and he realised it. 'Oh, hell, why don't you tell me to shut up and mind my own business?' he exclaimed disgustedly.

'Shut up and mind your own business, Greg,' she said, and her gay laughter trilled out, catching the attention of Will who was on his way to the bunkhouse and causing him to stop and stare for a moment at the two young people standing close together beside the dinghy.

The sail down the loch and back again was a success. Gina and Gregor took turns at the tiller and at jib-handling and were soon working together as a team. When he was leaving to return to the castle in Andrea's two-seater, Gregor asked her if they might sail together again the next day.

'If the weather is suitable I don't see why we shouldn't,' she replied, aware that Will was standing at the front door watching.

'And will you ask Will if I can help him with the camp?' was the next question, asked appealingly.

'Now that is something *you* must do for yourself,' she said, and he made a face at her before slipping into gear and roaring off in a cloud of dust.

That evening for the first time in days, Lachie did not come for the evening meal. He had gone to Ullapool, driven there by Will, who said he would go in later to pick him up and bring him back to the glen.

As they ate their meal Gina noticed that Will was very quiet. She supposed he was always quiet at that time of the day, but she hadn't noticed because of Lachie's presence at the table. Certainly breakfast was never a quiet meal because Will was always lively in the morning, banging on her door to wake her up and then making outrageous remarks about her inability to get up early in the morning of her own accord.

She sat there wondering what she should talk about, growing more and more aware of tension. When she glanced up at last she found he was staring at her almost as if he had never seen her before. He had often stared at her, sometimes speculatively, sometimes with mischief dancing in his eyes, sometimes curiously, but she had never known him stare at her with such intensity before. It seemed as if a blue fire glowed in his eyes. Disconcerted, she burst suddenly into speech—anything to break the silence which had become unbearable.

'Gregor and I had a lovely sail today. Those dinghies handle very easily. What design are they?'

He blinked, looked away and answered her absently.

'You didn't mind us taking one out?' she asked, rather timidly. It hadn't occurred to her before that he might be annoyed about her taking the dinghy, without asking his permission first.

'No. You seemed to be handling it quite competently. How did Gregor manage?'

'He sails well. Will, don't you think he's getting better? Don't you see a difference in him this past week?'

'I'd be blind if I didn't,' he said drily. 'But then he's having a good time of it. He has a pretty young woman to talk to and sail with, all the home-made cakes and scones he can eat. There aren't many who have it so good. Better watch your step, George. He'll be falling in love with you next and then you'll be in a fix, and you an *engaged* woman.'

She decided to ignore that crack, although she wondered what had caused him to make it. It seemed to her that the dryness in his voice had verged on bitterness for a moment.

'He'd like to help you with the next camp,' she said quietly, watching him carefully for his reaction.

He looked at her sardonically.

'Then he'll have to ask me himself, won't he?' he said.

'That's what I told him. But you'll let him, won't you? I think it would do him good. You see, he wants to prove to

126

you that he can do something positive, and you said that when he felt like that he'd be making progress.'

'Prove to me?' he queried, raising one eyebrow. 'I thought it was you he wants to impress.'

'It was at first, but now it's you.'

'I'll believe that when he comes and asks me if he can help,' he replied, still sardonic. 'It seems he's succeeded where you are concerned and you're suitably impressed. Isn't that so?'

She looked at him, her golden eyes wide and slightly puzzled. In the glow from the oil lamp her skin had a creamy sheen and the red in her hair glinted. Although she did not realise it, the weeks in the glen had brought her latant beauty into full bloom.

'I'm not sure what you mean. I like Gregor very much,' she said slowly.

'Well, that's a start, isn't it?' he remarked, pushing his chair away from the table and leaning back in it so that his face was in the shadow. 'I'd say it's a sign you're almost recovered. Do you ever think of Noll these days?'

She hadn't thought of Oliver for days, but as she reached for an empty plate she noticed the ring on her finger.

'When I notice his ring,' she retorted sharply.

'Then perhaps you should get rid of it,' he suggested softly.

'When the camp is over, not before,' she replied, rising to her feet and taking the plates over to the sink. She returned to the table with the pie she had made. She cut it into wedges aware that he was watching her again. He was in a strange mood, she thought. If anyone ever asked her in the future if she had known Will Fox, she would never be able to answer with a straight unqualified affirmative. It would take years to get to know him.

He took the plate she passed to him and set it down on the table in front of him.

'I shall miss your cooking when you go,' he said.

'Not me, just my cooking?' she challenged lightly. She

did not wish to think about leaving the glen, not yet, and it seemed to her that he was wishing to get rid of her.

He didn't answer her challenge, but began to talk about how he intended to organise the next camp. He asked for her opinion, which she gave, but all the time she had the feeling he was discussing the camp because he wished to keep away from any further intimate or personal conversation. When he had finished eating he helped her clear the table and then went off to the living room to answer some letters.

After pottering about the kitchen for a while, Gina realised she was doing nothing really except putting off the moment when she would go into the living room too, to sit and sew. It was silly to behave in this way just because she was alone with Will in the house. They had been alone before and she hadn't felt this oddly restless feeling.

She went up to her room and glanced out of the window. Spring had brought longer days with it and light still lingered in the sky behind the mountain. Gina sighed involuntarily as she felt her blood stir. So far it had been an untasted spring for her because her love had been snatched away from her by an untimely death.

She looked down at Oliver's ring and thought of the strange conversation she had just had with Oliver's brother. What had he meant when he had said she should get rid of the ring which tied her not only to Oliver but by a strange freak of circumstance tied her to Will too. If she had not worn the ring Gregor would not have assumed she was engaged to Will and the whole complication would not have happened. Was it possible that Will was finding his pseudo engagement to her irksome? Had he been suggesting that if she got rid of the ring he would be rid of her?

It was useless to let herself be tortured by such questions. She would go and ask him outright. Picking up her embroidery, she went down to the living room and sat near the small table where the second oil lamp had been placed. Will was still at his desk. He had not looked up when she had entered.

With Blue curled at her feet, Gina pushed the needle in and out of the canvas seat cover. All was quiet except for the purring of the kitten and the scratching of Will's pen on paper. Then that noise stopped too. She looked up. Will wasn't writing any more, but was leaning back in his chair and staring at her as he had stared at her in the kitchen. She moved a little uneasily, as he stood up and walked slowly over to her.

'What are you doing?' he asked.

'Petit point.'

'What is it for?'

She spread the embroidery out on her lap. The formalised design of roses glowed in the lamplight.

'It's a cover for the seat of a dining-room chair. Mother gave me a set of reproduction Regency chairs for a wedding present,' she replied.

'Are you always going to let the past dog you?' he asked suddenly. 'Wearing a ring which means nothing, sewing a seat cover on which he'll never sit. You're young and beautiful, and it's time you came alive.'

The seat cover was snatched from her knee and flung across the room. The violent action startled the kitten, which reared up and clawed at Will's trousers, was picked up and dropped on to the seat of another armchair.

Gina, astonished by Will's behaviour, was on her feet without realising it.

'Will Fox, your manners are atrocious!' she spluttered.

He grinned down at her, and she became aware that she was trapped between him and the chair on which she had been sitting.

'Yes, they are, aren't they?' he conceded. 'That's why my mother tries to pretend I don't exist. I might embarrass her some day. It's also why Noll didn't want me to attend his wedding. Did you know he wrote to me saying he didn't expect me to accept the invitation you had sent, and that he'd understand if I refused? If I'd come to the ceremony he'd have been on pins all the time in case I made some awful gaffe. And now, George, I'm going to give you another taste of my atrocious manners.'

He jerked her forward roughly and kissed her. Unlike the last time she didn't pull away from him, acknowledging ruefully that this was what she had been wanting him to do. Giving in to the desire which flared suddenly within her, she responded, holding him closely, luxuriating in the warmth and possessiveness of his embrace.

After a while, still holding her, he rubbed his cheek against the silkiness of her hair and whispered into her ear.

'Aren't you going to say "How dare you?"' he asked mockingly.

'No.' Her voice was shaky. 'But I'm beginning to wonder if you've let yourself be carried away by the part you're playing.'

He laughed and his arms tightened about her.

'You know what the next step is?' he queried suggestively.

'Yes.' She tried to move away from him.

'Do you want to take it with me?' he asked.

Her whole body stiffened in reaction and he released her at once.

'Don't panic, George,' he said, suddenly cool. 'We'll take it slowly. After all, that's what an engagement is for, isn't it? Though it seems to me Noll didn't use his time very well. You are ridiculously innocent for your age and only half alive.'

'But we're not engaged,' she retorted frantically, appalled at the way her senses were clamouring for him to take her in his arms again.

'In the eyes of our immediate neighbours, we are,' he reminded her, and there was a touch of steel in his voice. 'It struck me today that young Gregor was becoming suspicious and that maybe we ought to behave in a more lover-like way when he's about the place. I'm going to fetch Lachie now. Be sure you're in your bed before I get back, won't you?'

His mockery flickered her on the raw. With a toss of her head she turned away to look for her embroidery. She could hear him whistling his tantalising tune, then the front door closed and she was alone in the silence of the house.

She made sure she was in bed before he returned. In her room she buried the embroidery at the bottom of one of her suitcases: She would not sew again while she was staying at White Lodge. She was also tempted to remove Oliver's ring from her finger and put it in its velvet-lined box at the bottom of the suitcase too, but the thought of the remarks its absence from her finger might bring forth stopped her.

Once in bed she closed her eyes determined to sleep, but for the first time since she had come to the glen sleep avoided her. She was fidgety and restless, thinking about Will, of the quick searching ruthlessness of his kiss which had discovered her innocence, of the roughness of his cheek against hers, of the warmth of his hands and body. Oliver had never kissed her like that, and the trouble was she had wanted it to continue, had longed to take the next step.

But how could she take any step which would involve her with Will when there was always the shadow of Bridget hovering in the background? How could she go any further with him without love in her heart?

And she wasn't in love with Will. Nor was he in love with her, and what had happened down there in the lamplit dusk of the living room had been merely the result of the spring, the time of the year when, as everyone knew, the fancy turns to thoughts of love.

CHAPTER FIVE

'AND what makes you think you can help me? As far as I can see you've been nothing else but a parasite ever since you came into this world.'

Will's voice had that abrasive quality with which Gina was only too familiar. Memory of the first time they had met in her flat came flooding back. She felt herself cringing inwardly, a feeling which was followed almost immediately by a strong desire to strike back at him.

But he wasn't speaking to her. He was speaking to Gregor who had come at last to ask if he could help at the next camp. It had taken him two days to pluck up the courage to ask Will, and now he was there outside the kitchen window which Gina had opened to let in the fresh morning air.

Holding her breath, she waited for him to answer Will's searing attack. Would he retaliate or would he run away?

'I can sail.' He said that confidently enough. Then came the staggering challenge. 'I bet I can climb the cliffs at the mouth of the loch in a faster time than you can.'

A cold hand seemed to clutch at Gina's heart. Surely Will wouldn't take up that challenge. The thought of them clinging to that wall of rock, high above the foaming water, horrified her.

'Do you now?' Will's voice had changed. It sounded amused, interested. 'All right. Are you game to try this morning?'

'Yes. Only I haven't any boots,' said Gregor hesitantly.

'The weather has been dry, so those plimsolls you're wearing will do,' replied Will easily. 'I'll ask George to come and stand at the top of the cliffs to time us and see who reaches the top first. Does that sound fair to you?'

Again Gregor's answer was a nervously spoken agreement and Gina had a desire to scream through the window, 'No, you mustn't. You'll both be killed.'

By the time they came into the kitchen to tell her their plan and to ask for her co-operation, she had controlled her desire to scream at them, but she was still pale and she stated her opinion of them concisely.

'I think you're both crazy, and I refuse to do what you ask.'

Will laughed at her.

'A purely feminine reaction,' he said, flicking her cheek with his fingers, an action which did not go unnoticed by Gregor. 'Come on, now, sweetheart. Be at the top to greet the winner with a kiss. We'll climb without you even if you won't come, but it won't be half so much fun without a reward, will it, Gregor?'

Gregor swallowed nervously, smiled a trifle wanly and agreed that it would not be so much fun without the promised kiss as a reward.

Will took a bunch of keys out of his pocket, chose one of them and held it out to Gregor.

'Here, take this. It opens the door of the storeroom in the first bunkhouse. You'll find ropes there. Bring two. I think we should both take one in case we need them. While you're gone I'll try and persuade George that she'll miss a great adventure if she doesn't come and then I'll ask Lachie to come with us to the bottom of the cliff with us to say "go".'

It was the first time he had ever spoken to Gregor as if he considered him to be a rational intelligent person and the young man noticed and reacted accordingly.

'I'll go right away,' he said, taking the key. Then with a smile in Gina's direction he added, 'Be ready with that kiss, Gina, when I reach the top of the cliff first.'

Alone with Will, Gina turned on him.

'You can't let him do it. His nerves are still bad.'

'He issued the challenge, remember,' he replied coldly. 'You once said he wanted to prove himself. Well, this is his chance.'

'But those cliffs are so dangerous,' she quavered.

'They're not as bad as they look,' he said.

'Not to you, perhaps, but you're an experienced rock-climber and assault leader. Gregor isn't.'

'If he isn't able to climb that rock then he should never have challenged me,' he retorted. 'If he fails it will prove better than anything else would that he's unsuitable to help at the camp and that he's not able to take responsibility. On the other hand, if he makes it to the top in front of me or behind me, I'll be willing to have him as an instructor.'

He was hard and ice-cold. This was the side of him Gina disliked heartily and could never like. It had been developed by his service in the Army, she realised, and was the reason why he would always be a leader and not a follower.

Her dislike showed in her face and made her eyes shimmer with green-shot golden light. He returned her gaze coolly, completely unmoved.

'Oh, you're so hard!' she exclaimed. 'No wonder Bridget ran away from you. Being married to you must have been like being married to a piece of granite!'

She might just as well have kept her mouth shut for all the effect her words had on him.

'*You* wanted him cured,' he said curtly. 'Well, he is, almost.'

'But supposing he falls?'

'He won't because he'll know that you're waiting at the top to greet him with a kiss when he comes roaring over the edge,' he retorted drily. 'See you there in about an hour and a half.'

An hour and twenty minutes Gina stood at the top of the cliffs. Behind her several sheep and their lambs grazed on the short sweet grass which carpeted the rocky headland jutting out into the sea and forming one side of the entrance to Loch Gorm.

Peering cautiously over the edge, she could see no one climbing the sheer rock which flashed pink in the sunshine.

About twenty feet below she could see a small ledge and wondered if it was the one from which Will had rescued Blue. But when she looked away to the right and then to the left she realised that the cliffs were so extensive that there could be many small ledges. Here and there small bushes and stunted trees grew out of crevices and she wondered how they managed to survive in such a wild windswept place.

It was a lovely day and when she turned away from the edge of the cliff she could see far out to sea to a line of land on the horizon, dark blue and mountainous. She guessed it was a distant Hebridean island. High above the sky was a pale washed-out blue, across which small clouds were drifting. Far below the water heaved and rippled, glinting with reflected light.

Turning back, she peered over the edge of the cliff in time to see Gregor reach the ledge. She told herself she was glad he was ahead of Will. Although it was just five minutes short of the time Will had said it would take him to climb the cliff, there was no sign of him. Jamming her hands into the pockets of her suede jacket, she turned her back on the cliff and looked out to sea again.

Keeping her gaze fixed on three fishing boats which were chugging steadily north, she forced her mind away from pictures of Will lying unconscious somewhere with a broken limb or crushed ribs. Or Will hurtling down into the fangs of the turbulent water at the foot of the cliffs. It was Gregor she should be worrying about, not Will. Gregor, who was young, soft and easily hurt like herself, not Will, who was as hard as the rock he was climbing.

Two hands curved round her waist. She stiffened as if an electric shock had shot through her. The hands slipped across her body and she was pulled against a wide chest which was rising and falling rhythmically after recent exertion.

'I've come for the reward,' Will whispered laughingly in her ear.

135

She twisted in his arms to face him. He gave her no chance to say anything, but took the reward before she had offered it.

'I didn't see you,' she exclaimed when he released her at last from that ruthless embrace. 'I thought Gregor would be first.'

'I was further over to the east of him. Are you disappointed?' She shook her head, her bruised mouth slightly tremulous.

'No. Only very glad to see you safe,' she whispered, betraying her recent anxiety on his behalf.

'You're coming on, George,' he mocked, then turned as, with a scrabbling sound of shod feet against rock, Gregor heaved himself pantingly over the edge of the cliff and lay there laughing breathlessly in the sunshine.

'I did it. I did it!' he cried exultantly. 'I knew I could!'

He rolled over and sprang lithely to his feet. With his dark hair blowing about his flushed face, his black eyes sparkling with triumph and his white teeth showing in a triumphant grin, he was suddenly the epitome of vigorous attractive youth, and Gina felt the strong pull of his attraction.

'I suppose Will has taken his reward,' he said ruefully.

'Yes, he has,' she replied, smiling at him, 'but you're going to be *given* one.'

Reaching up, she put her arms round his neck. He responded instantly. His lips were warm and sweet against her own and his arms held her close as he recognised the spontaneity of her kiss.

'Break it up,' urged Will drily. 'You have another spectator besides me. Lachie is coming, and he has a way of telling tales around the countryside.'

Gregor sprang away from Gina as if he were guilty of some grave misdemeanour, and Gina turned to see Lachie loping across the grass towards them.

'Ach, that was a fine effort, lad, just fine,' he said as he clapped Gregor on the shoulder. 'Sure and I knew you'd be doing it in record time. I mind the day when I climbed a cliff like that. In the summer of forty-one, it was. I was doing my Commando training near Ben Nevis and...'

'You didn't come here to tell us about your assault training during the last war,' Will interrupted him rather impatiently.

'So I haven't,' agreed Lachie mildly. 'There is a young woman down at the house asking for you by your first name. She's come in a wee grey car.'

For the second time that morning Gina felt as if icy fingers had seized her heart. Had Bridget come back? She glanced at Will. His face was as impassive as usual, but mockery twinkled in his eyes as they met hers as if he had guessed at her thought and was amused by her consternation.

'Then I must go and see who this young woman is,' he murmured, and he set off down the well-worn path towards the house.

'Wait!' commanded Gregor, hurrying after Will. 'Are you going to let me help at the camp?'

Together, he and Will went down the path. Matching her step to Lachie's lope, Gina followed them, reluctant to face the woman who had come and had asked for Will by his first name.

As they approached the house she could see the woman pacing beside a grey Volkswagen. She was tall and blonde and from a distance she looked rather like Birdie, not at all like the picture Gina had seen of Bridget. With relief surging through her, Gina watched the woman turn, see Will and hurry towards him with her arms outstretched. They met, their arms going round each other in an affectionate embrace. Gina's steps faltered for a moment, but she couldn't retreat because Lachie was there clucking his tongue and asking her whether she was going to stand for yon man kissing another woman like that. Greg was also looking at her, presumably wondering how she was reacting to that fond greeting.

137

By the time she reached the grey car the embrace was over and the woman was talking to Will in German, the words pouring out excitedly, her white teeth flashing in her tanned face.

Will turned to Gina and smiled. There was affection in that smile and he reached out his hand to her. She put hers into it, glad to feel the warm comfort of his grasp.

'Come and meet Irma Brandt, an old friend of mine from my time in Germany,' he said, and in a daze she heard him introducing her for the second time as his fiancée.

Smiling, Gina held out her hand and welcomed Irma who, looking slightly disconcerted, responded vaguely in attractively-accented English and then shot a sharp question in German at Will, who answered lazily in the same language. Then he added in English,

'No one else speaks German here, Irma, so you'll have to practise your English. Let's go into the house. I'm in great need of liquid refreshment after climbing that cliff and I expect Gregor is too. How far have you come today?'

His arm round Gina's waist he urged her forward into the house. Once in the hallway Gina turned into the kitchen and suggested that he and Irma went into the living room and she would bring refreshments to them. Gregor, however, followed her into the kitchen.

'That was a surprise all round, wasn't it?' he remarked, sitting on the table and swinging his legs.

'What do you mean?' asked Gina cautiously as she prepared to make coffee for herself and Irma.

'Surprise for Will, surprise for you and surprise for Irma,' he replied.

'I didn't realise Will was surprised. I thought he behaved as if he was pleased to see her.'

'Do I detect a note of jealousy?' mocked Gregor. 'Because someone out of your fiancé's past love-life has turned up?'

'What makes you think she's been one of his loves?' asked Gina sharply.

'I'm just guessing from the expression on her face when he introduced you as his fiancée. For a moment she looked as if she'd been shot down in flames.'

'Oh, dear. What a muddle!' sighed Gina.

'Why do you say that?'

Her remark had sprung from genuine regret that her pseudo-engagement to Will might be causing more unhappiness, and she was now so used to Gregor being with her that she had forgotten he did not know the truth.

'I don't like being the cause of unhappiness for others,' she explained rather lamely, aware he was watching her with bright observant eyes.

'I was rather puzzled by something she said to him after he had introduced you to her. Did you notice? She spoke to him in German,' mused Gregor.

'Do you know German? Oh, tell me, what did she say?' asked Gina.

'I'm not fluent in the language, but I did study it at school and I've been to Germany on a couple of holidays. She said something about not having realised he was free, and how long he had been free. It made me wonder whether he'd been in prison at some time.'

'Don't be silly. Of course he hasn't. What answer did he make?'

'He was non-committal, I thought. He said he'd been free quite a while and then suggested she spoke in English. He wasn't pleased by the question.'

Had the question referred to Bridget? Had Irma been asking how long Will had been free to become engaged and marry again? And did his answer mean he was no longer married to Bridget?

'Any idea what they were talking about?' prompted Gregor.

'No, not at all. But I expect Will will tell me later. Would you like to have some beer and take him some before he comes in here roaring for it. I'll follow with coffee as soon as it's ready. Did Lachie come in?'

139

'No. He hasn't taken to Irma. Said she was an incomer and he doesn't hold with incomers.'

'Then what does he think I am?' exclaimed Gina.

'You came with the swans and so you are the true mistress of the master of the glen. Had you forgotten?' said Gregor with a chuckle. Then, unable to keep his own concerns to himself any longer, he burst out with his news. 'Will is going to let me help with the camp. I'm to start this morning, looking over the rigging of the dinghies and making sure it's all in good order, and inspecting the canoes for holes. He even suggested that I move into the bunkhouse and come and take my meals here before the camp starts on Monday.'

'Are you pleased?'

'Yes, I'm pleased, although that's rather an understatement of the way I feel after climbing that cliff this morning. I'm very pleased, thanks to you, Gina.'

'And to Will,' she insisted, worried by the ardent expression in his eyes.

'Thanks to you both, then, but I can't help wishing...'

He stopped talking abruptly in mid-sentence and immediately she was curious.

'Can't help wishing what?' she asked.

'That you weren't engaged to him.'

'Oh, Gregor,' she wailed, 'don't you start! Everything is in such a muddle as it is. What am I going to do?'

'You mean you're not sure any more whether you want to be engaged to Will?' he asked eagerly.

'I'm not sure about anything any more,' she said a little wildly. 'Now go and take this beer into the other room.'

After drinking his beer and listening a little while longer to Irma's discourse on all the places she had visited during the extended holiday she had taken, Will excused himself and took Gregor with him. As he left the room he kissed Gina on the cheek, to keep up appearances, of course, suggested to her that Irma might like to stay for the day, then went out trailing a rather thunderous-looking Gregor behind him.

Gina found it easy to entertain the unexpected visitor, who was interested in everything to do with the farm and talked enough for two. They went to feed the swans and lingered on the shore beside the rippling water. The silent mountain basked tranquilly in the sunshine, its cap of ice gradually diminishing in size, and the moors glowed purple and gold.

'You will not mind if I say something a little personal to you, Gina?' asked Irma.

Gina glanced sideways at her companion. In the clear light she could see faint lines under Irma's smooth make-up. The woman was older than she had at first thought, nearer to Will's age than to her own.

'No. At least I don't think so. How can I tell until you've said it?' she countered, with a laugh.

Irma joined in the laughter, throwing her head back, her white teeth flashing, her blonde hair glinting metallically. She was a vigorous person who did everything with great gusto.

'That's true,' she agreed. 'Then I will say it. I find it strange that you are living here alone with Will before you are married. Is it the custom?'

In spite of her resolve not to let herself be disconcerted by anything Irma might say, Gina felt the blood seeping slowly into her cheeks.

'No, it isn't. I came to stay here and to help with the cooking for the Easter camp. When we arrived we found that his partner had walked out on him, taking with him his wife who usually did the cooking. Will asked me if I would stay just the same and help him until he found someone else. I could hardly refuse, could I?'

'But why didn't you marry straight away?'

Gina was a little flustered by this question and wondered uneasily whether it had already been out to Will and what his answer had been.

'Why don't you ask Will?' she countered.

Irma's high shoulders rose in a shrug.

'I ask him many questions which he does not answer. He is very good at, how do you say it? At the fencing. I hoped you would be more straightforward.'

'Then I say that we did not marry immediately because we did not wish to. An engagement is a time to get to know one another better before taking an extremely important step. And that's what Will and I are doing. We're getting to know one another,' replied Gina, her thoughts winging back to Will's easy and slow philosophy. Little had she guessed that she would be using it in self-defence.

'I see. I can understand Will wishing to be careful this time. His first marriage was such a disaster, wasn't it?' said Irma.

'I don't know. He never talks about it. Did you know Bridget?'

'No. She had left him before I met him. I was his German teacher. It was a language course for young Army officers. Will was my best pupil. He has a very good ear for language. Ah, we had many happy times together in Luneburg,' Irma sighed reminiscently. 'After he left the Army we kept in touch, through letters. I hoped that one day he would be free. He told me nothing of you in his letters,' she added sharply.

Gina hoped that the expression on her face was not giving her away as she thought of the letters, written in German on pink perfumed paper, which she had found amongst the other correspondence in Will's desk. There was a vague similarity between this conversation and the one she had once held with Andrea. Yet Irma was no adolescent with a schoolgirl crush on a man much older than herself. She was a mature woman who had seen her hopes dashed that morning when Will had introduced his new fiancée to her; hopes that one day, when he was free of Bridget, she could become his wife.

'I'm sorry,' Gina muttered, as she had once apologised to

142

Andrea. At the first opportunity she must speak to Will and tell him that the pseudo-engagement was over. It was causing too many complications. 'You must stay here for the rest of your holiday,' she suggested impulsively.

Irma glanced at her, puzzlement shadowing her clear grey eyes.

'Thank you. I would like to do that,' she said slowly. 'I'm very fond of Will and I would not like to see him make the same mistake again.'

'What do you mean?'

'Please forgive me for being frank. It is my nature to say what I think. You seem soft and helpless, as I believe Bridget was, lying in wait to catch a man like Will, who is strong and confident and so often compassionate towards those who are weaker than he is. He was caught by that helplessness once before, and I have read that a man often falls for the same type of woman over and over again. I shall stay here for a while and make sure that he is not going to make the same mistake twice.'

Irma turned away and walked back to the house. Alone, Gina finished feeding the swans. She found she was shaking with anger. Soft and helpless like Bridget, was she? And that was why Will had taken pity on her and had brought her to the glen to recover from the shock of Oliver's death. Was it also the reason why he had asked her to take the next step with him the other night? Had he wanted her only because she reminded him of Bridget?

It was a thought she could not bear. She must find out what had happened to Bridget and why Will was free of her.

Irma stayed for lunch and spent the afternoon following Will around the farm. She left before the evening meal to return to Ullapool where she was staying the night in the hotel.

'Irma tells me you've invited her to stay here,' said Will as he helped Gina to clear away dishes after the evening meal was over. 'It's a good idea. She can help you with the

143

cooking while the campers are here.'

'I'd rather she didn't,' replied Gina, more sharply than she had intended, and he gave her a searching sidelong glance.

'Why?' he asked.

'You know the saying about too many cooks,' she retorted.

'I do. But I thought you'd like some help. After all, it's very hard work and this time there'll be thirty campers.'

'Didn't I manage all right for the last camp?'

'You did. Remarkably well considering you were not exactly up to scratch after the shock you'd had,' he murmured placatingly.

'I may look soft and helpless,' she rushed on, 'but I can assure you that I'm not. I'm not like Bridget.'

'No one knows that better than I do,' he said quietly, his face like stone, his eyes two pools of blue ice. 'Who said you're like her?'

'Irma did.'

'Why were you discussing Bridget with her?' he demanded frostily.

'Oh, because she brought up the subject that you'd been married before.' Then seeing his face darken with anger she went on, 'Oh, Will, don't you think I should leave now and jilt you? This phoney engagement is creating such a lot of complications.'

'No.' The negative came out forcibly and called her to order. She looked at him rather timidly and waited.

With an effort he smiled at her.

'Sorry to bark at you, but I had to make you pay attention somehow. Now listen to me. We shall keep up this phoney engagement, as you call it, at least until the campers have gone. After that you can leave if you wish to.'

'But I can't see how it's helping anyone.'

'It's helping me. You can take my word for that.'

She glanced at him dubiously. He smiled at her and

lifted her left hand from her side and looked down at the ring.

'Thanks to poor old Noll, this makes the engagement look convincing to outsiders, even though it would not be my choice for you. Has anyone ever told you that when you're upset or angry your eyes blaze like topazes, sweetheart?'

'Will, stop making fun,' she said huskily, pulling her hand from his.

'I'm not.'

'I wish I knew what game you're playing.'

'A waiting game,' he murmured. 'Easy and slow. Remember? Are you going to do as I ask?'

'Only if you'll tell me about Bridget, please. I think I've a right to know.'

He turned away from her to put some dishes away in a cupboard. He came back to her and put his hands on her shoulders, holding her so that she had to look up at him. His mouth was set in a grim line and his eyes were shadowed, reminding her of the way he had looked the night he had told her he had a twinge of pain from an old wound.

'If I tell you will you promise to keep it all to yourself?' he asked gravely.

'I promise.'

'Then come into the other room. We may as well be comfortable while I unfold the details of my lurid past.'

His self-mockery did not mislead her. He was about to tell her about something which had hurt him, she was sure of that; something which had bruised his emotions, driving them underground; something which had made him what he was now, a little tough and enigmatic in his dealings with women.

In the living room she sat on the window seat and looked out. Down on the loch one swan swam, a lonely shape silhouetted against the golden water. The woods were dark now, the shapes of the trees blurred. Beyond them the moors still reflected the radiance of the setting sun and Ben

145

Searg's sharp summit was violet, laced with silver, glinting against the pale evening sky.

Will searched in his desk, throwing crumpled paper to the floor, muttering something about having to tidy it one day. Gina hid a smile, thinking of how many times he said that and did nothing, leaving her to attempt to make order out of chaos.

At last, finding what he wanted, he came across to her and tossed a long buff envelope on to her lap.

'Read that,' he ordered tersely. 'I'll fill in the background when I've locked up the hens.'

He went out of the room. Gina stared at the envelope. It was addressed to Will at White Lodge. Her throat tight with apprehension, she drew out the single sheet of paper which the envelope contained. The heading on the paper was the address of a hospital in the south of England and the date was the seventeenth of August four years previously.

Quickly she read the letter. In terse direct terms it informed Captain Fox of the death of his wife Bridget and requested him to attend her funeral. After that announcement the language of the letter changed slightly as if the writer of it, a certain Dr Lilian Vance, had known Will personally. She assured him that everything had been done for his wife and that he must never blame himself for the condition into which she had sunk, but should regard her death as a blessing in disguise because she had been hopelessly and incurably addicted.

Her hands shaking, Gina folded the sheet of paper and replaced it in the envelope. Bridget was dead, and had been for almost four years. She had been a drug addict and had presumably been in a mental hospital. Suddenly, quite clearly, Gina could see and hear Will as he had looked and spoken in her bedroom at the flat when he'd asked her if she had taken a drug to escape from reality. Now she understood what had been behind his jeer. Now she understood, also, his silence on the subject of Bridget, so that even Meg,

146

who had known Bridget, still did not know she was dead or how she had died.

Will re-entered the room and sat down beside her.

'I'm so sorry,' she murmured.

'Don't be. It wasn't much of a marriage. I married her for all the wrong reasons,' he replied grimly.

'What were they?' she asked.

'Pity, a wish to help someone weaker than myself. It's always been one of my shortcomings and verges on arrogance, I suppose. Add to that physical desire and you have a bad mixture,' he replied cynically.

'Meg told me that you met Bridget at her home.'

'Yes. I was on leave and interested only in having a good time. She was pretty and also interested in a good time. She was easy to make love to—too easy. I took what she offered, went back to Germany and never gave her another thought. Then she ran away from the Maxwells'. She told me afterwards she found their way of life too strict. Six months later she turned up in Germany and begged me to marry her. I told her to go home to Scotland, but she wouldn't. She threatened to commit suicide if I didn't marry her. I didn't realise then what was wrong with her and, as I still found her physically attractive, I married her and created my own hell.'

'But why did she run away from you?' asked Gina.

'I discovered that she was helping to smuggle drugs from Holland into Germany. I threatened to expose her to the police if she didn't stop, so she ran away. Sickened and disillusioned by then, not only by her bad habits but also by her inability to love anyone other than herself, I told myself that I didn't care. I let two years slip by without trying to find her. Then Meg wrote to me asking why she hadn't received any letters from either Bridget or myself and I realised I would have to try and find her.'

'Where did you start to look?'

'It wasn't difficult, because in the meantime I received a letter from that hospital. She had been taken there after a suicide attempt while under the influence of drugs. I went to see her. She was in a pitiful state. They said there was hope for her if I'd take her back and provide her with a good home, somewhere in the country, they suggested, away from the city and all its distractions. A farm with animals she could take an interest in. Sympathy and kindness was what she needed, they said. Remembering what she'd been like, I didn't really believe them, but I did as they suggested. What else could I do? I'd married her. She was my wife for better or for worse, and even though I didn't love her I couldn't desert her just then, because she had no one else.' He stopped talking abruptly, his voice choked with bitterness.

'So you found the glen,' said Gina softly.

'Yes, and bought it and went to work in Ullapool, thinking that it was possible, when the hospital released her and allowed her to come north, she would soon recover in such peaceful surroundings where nature is all-important. Then that letter came. It was all over and I had only the future to look forward to. My marriage was an ugly mess which I preferred to forget. I couldn't even talk about it to anyone, not even Meg. You're the first to know.'

'Thank you for telling me.'

'Does it help you to know?' he asked, taking the letter from her and going over to the desk to push it into a pigeonhole.

'Of course it does. I've been terribly worried in case she turned up unexpectedly and found us "engaged".'

'You shouldn't have been. I thought I'd told you she wouldn't be coming back.'

'Yes, but you didn't say why she wouldn't be coming back and your attitude didn't make it easy to ask questions. Why have you kept it all hidden, Will? Wouldn't it have been better to tell someone?' she queried.

He moved away from the desk and came to stand beside her.

'That's a hard one to answer,' he murmured. 'I suppose

the answer lies somewhere in my nature. I've always tended to keep my problems and my failures to myself, and my marriage to Bridget was a problem and a failure from start to finish. In being too sympathetic towards her when she came to me in Germany I almost destroyed myself as well as contributing to her destruction. If I'd been tougher with her from the start we would never have married and it's just possible she might have survived.'

He murmured something about having to go and see Lachie and went from the room, leaving Gina to stare out at the shadows deepening in the glen.

The next day Irma returned and moved into the bedroom which had been the Andersons' when they had lived at White Lodge. She said she would stay for as long as the campers were there in order to give Will some help. She was a Girl Guide leader and had had much experience in camping and in the use of the compass. She also knew some geology and was willing to give talks on the subject to the campers. Will seemed very pleased to have her there and had no compunction in making use of her.

Later the same day Gregor arrived in Andrea's car and moved into one of the bunkhouses, and that evening there were four for supper in the big kitchen at White Lodge. The long quiet evenings were over.

On Monday the campers arrived. This time they were a mixed bunch, mostly young men whose ages ranged from seventeen to twenty-five. They came not only from Britain but also from different parts of the continent, and after their arrival there was no more time for personal conversations between Gina and the other inmates of the house.

The days passed by quickly, sometimes sunny and mild, sometimes grey and boisterous as the wind whipped the water and shook the trees. Sea-birds driven inshore by the wild weather shrieked and chattered as they circled and hovered over the loch and surrounding fields and moors. In the garden, obeying the summons of the season, huge purple flowers bloomed on the rhododendron bushes and the two laburnum trees dripped yellow blossoms.

Gina cooked meals, packed up lunches, organised washing-up parties and gave instruction in sailing. Every night she fell into bed and slept deeply. During the day she was aware of Gregor, smiling and growing more confident by the hour; of Irma and Will laughing and joking together in German as they enjoyed each other's company.

Towards the end of the second week of the camp she began to think about leaving. In a few days she could leave, if she wished. Will would not bind her.

The thought of leaving made her heart ache in a strange way, yet the more she saw of Will and Irma together the more convinced she became that she was in the way of their happiness. Once the camp was over she would break off her pseudo-engagement to Will, return to Birmingham and take up the thread of her life again from where it had been broken before her real engagement to Oliver.

The necessity for her to leave soon was brought home to her by a letter from Meg Maxwell, who had already written to Will to tell him that she and her husband were taking a few days' holiday and would call to see him. She had written separately to Gina to say she had heard that Will's 'chief cook and bottle-washer' was still with him and that she looked forward to meeting her again.

The letter came as a slight shock, but a necessary one. It would never do for Meg to come and find her engaged to Will, Gina decided. It was all very well keeping up an act for the benefit of neighbours and outsiders, but it would never do to deceive someone belonging to Will's family. There she drew the line, even if he didn't. She would have to leave that week-end before the Maxwells arrived.

The sight of Irma and Will in close conversation as they returned slowly to the house in the dusk on the last evening of the camp confirmed her in her decision. She must leave before Irma did and give both Irma and Will the chance of happiness which had been denied them while Bridget had lived.

Such thoughts gave her no pleasure and that night she slept badly, with the result that she overslept and did not waken next morning until she felt a hand on her shoulder as someone shook her. She opened her eyes to find Will bending over her. Behind him bright sunlight streamed through the window.

'Oh. What's happened?' gasped Gina, sitting up in bed.

'You didn't hear me bang on the door,' he replied curtly.

'Oh, dear, the breakfast!' she said ruefully.

'Don't give it a thought. Irma is cooking it and doing a great job at such short notice. You should have let her help you with the cooking before this, then you wouldn't have become so tired.'

There was no sympathy in his attitude. He was just stating a matter of fact, and although she knew he was right Gina did not feel any better.

'She's welcome to cook here whenever she likes, all summer if she wishes,' she said haughtily, her chin up and her eyelids drooping. Then she wished she had kept quiet because his eyes began to gleam with mockery.

'She doesn't want to stay. She's leaving this afternoon,' he said calmly.

'I don't believe it. She told me she would stay here as long as she could,' she retorted.

His eyebrows went up in surprise, but all he said was,

'Well, she's stayed, and this afternoon she's leaving.'

'So am I,' announced Gina, rather breathlessly, and saw the mockery fade from his eyes as their expression sharpened.

'How?' he asked.

She nibbled her lower lip, in a quandary. How she would leave had not been one of the questions she had asked herself during the night and so she had no answer ready.

'With Irma, if there's no other way,' she said. 'I'm sure she'll be delighted to give me a lift.'

Will turned away from the bed and walked over to the door where he paused, his hand on the latch.

'I didn't think you'd be in such a hurry to leave,' he said. 'I hoped you'd stay a few days longer and meet Meg and Drew again. They'll be here by Monday afternoon.'

'And that's why I must leave soon. How can I stay when they're coming?'

He gave her a puzzled glance over his shoulder.

'I thought you liked Meg,' he murmured.

'I do, that's why I can't deceive her. We can't tell her we're engaged. She's your relative and she still believes Bridget is alive.'

'Perhaps the time has come for me to tell her about Bridget. Now that I've told you it won't be so difficult telling her,' he said slowly. 'Then she won't find our engagement strange.'

'But I don't want Meg to believe we're engaged,' she insisted rather desperately, wondering why he was being so obtuse. 'I don't want to deceive her. I want to go home.'

He turned back to the door and opened it slowly, apparently considering her rather wildly spoken request.

'All right,' he said at last. 'Then it shall be as you wish. Stay one more night and I promise that tomorrow I'll drive you south to catch a night train to Birmingham.'

He left the room closing the door behind him. Gina sat slumped on the bed, vaguely aware that something was wrong. Telling him that she wished to leave had been much easier than she had anticipated. One more night in the glen and her period of recuperation would be over. Oliver was not forgotten, but he was now part of a past which didn't hurt any more because the present and future were showing signs of being much more painful. She was well and whole again, but she had the most miserable feeling that she did not want to leave Glengorm after all. She wanted to stay here in the White Lodge and be chief cook and bottle-washer for its master.

When she went down to the kitchen she found Irma saying cheerful farewells to campers who were leaving and giving crisp guttural orders to those who were helping to clear away dishes. There was no doubt that she was in charge of the kitchen this morning.

'Your breakfast is in the oven,' she said to Gina after giving her a brisk good morning, and her cheerfulness grated on the nerves.

'Will tells me you're leaving today,' Gina said, taking the plate of food from the oven and placing it on the table. 'Couldn't you stay a little longer? I'm sure Will would like you to meet his aunt. She's coming here on Monday.'

'I would like to meet her very much. Will has told me how good she has been to him, making a home for him to go to when he was on leave from the army and he was not welcome in his mother's house,' said Irma, 'but I'm afraid I must return to Germany. I have liked it here. The glen is a beautiful place in which to live. I hope you realise how lucky you are. Excuse me, please.'

She left the room hurriedly. Alone, Gina ate her breakfast and thought. She was convinced that Irma had gone from the room quickly because she had been overcome with emotion at the thought of having to leave Will. Surely there must be some way in which she could help her to stay. If only she could leave that afternoon before the German woman, perhaps everything would work out happily after all. But how could she leave the glen and go south when she had no means of transport.

Just then Gregor came into the kitchen and she saw a way of solving her problem.

'I must speak to you alone somewhere,' she said to him. He looked surprised and then mischievous.

'You sound very mysterious,' he whispered. 'Come down to the loch where the dinghies are pulled up. My job for this morning is to make sure they're all intact. Maybe we could go for a sail. There's a small breeze wafting in from the sea.'

The small breeze, however, brought a smirring of rain with it so that Gina and Gregor were forced to retreat from the lochside to the shed where the dinghies, canoes and all their equipment were usually stored.

'We couldn't be more alone than we are here,' said Gregor. 'And there's no chance of us being disturbed by Will or Lachie because they've both gone to Ullapool this morning. What is it you want to tell me?'

'Ask, not tell,' Gina corrected him. 'Could you and would you take me to the nearest place where I could catch a train going south today?'

His black eyes widened and he whistled his surprise.

'I could and I would, but I'd like to know why,' he replied.

'I want to go to Birmingham,' she said.

He noted a certain tenseness in her manner and his eyes narrowed again, speculatively.

'Does Will know?' he queried warily.

'Yes, but he won't take me until tomorrow, and I want to go today.'

'Irma is leaving and should be driving through England. Why don't you ask her for a lift?' he suggested, looking thoroughly puzzled by now.

'I know she is, but you see I don't want her to leave. I want to stay here, and I think she will once I've gone,' replied Gina earnestly.

Gregor's expression of puzzlement changed to one of anxiety. He touched her forehead with his hand.

'Hot and feverish,' he announced. 'I guessed as much. You're not talking sense, Gina.'

'Yes, I am,' she insisted impatiently. 'At least it makes sense to me. Please will you do as I ask? Please, Gregor.'

'When you look at me like that I'm tempted to agree, out of hand,' he murmured. 'But I'm afraid of Will, so I'd like to know more before I do as you say. What's the matter? Are you fed up with Glengorm?'

'Yes.' Although her answer was far from the truth Gina seized on the reason he offered because she knew that it was one he would readily understand and accept. Other women had left the glen because they had been fed up with the way

154

of life there and Gregor knew that Madge Anderson had left for that reason.

'You can't be thinking of jilting Will,' Gregor said, hope lilting through his voice.

'Yes, I am,' she replied, gazing at him steadily, hoping that she sounded convincing and that the terrible ache of sadness she felt at the thought of leaving would not last too long.

'I can hardly believe it,' he murmured, and a strange little glow lit his dark eyes. 'Gina, say it's true and I'll drive you all the way to Birmingham,' he offered excitedly.

'It's true. Why are you so pleased?'

'Don't you see? You'll be free, and that gives me a chance. One day perhaps, you and I could . . .'

Aware that he was approaching closely, an ardent expression in his eyes as their glance shifted to her mouth, his arms reaching for her, Gina backed away from him.

'I'm not promising anything, Gregor,' she said sharply. 'Just help me to leave without Will knowing that I've gone.'

He lowered his arms to his sides but continued to stare at her intently.

'I don't understand,' he said. 'Are you sure you're doing the right thing by leaving?'

'Quite sure. You see, Irma is in love with Will and I think it's possible that he's in love with her. At any rate he's very fond of her. They're also very suited to each other. She's strong and clever and she knows all about camps and compasses, as well as how to cook, so she'd be a great asset to him in organising the camps. They've a great deal in common and have known each other for ages, much longer than he and I have known each other. Anyway I've decided that marriage between Will and me wouldn't work. After all, that's what an engagement is for, isn't it? To find out whether you're suited to one another before taking the next and most important step.'

Gina realised suddenly that she was babbling in her effort to convince Gregor and that he was looking even more worried and perplexed, so she stopped talking.

'I suppose you're right,' he murmured, but his manner lacked conviction. 'When would you like to leave?'

'As soon as possible after lunch. Oh, thank you, Gregor —I'm awfully grateful to you.'

A strange expression crossed his face and for a moment she had a brief impression of a different, rather malevolent Gregor. Then it passed and he gave her a twisted smile.

'You're very trusting, Gina. Knowing myself as I do I think I ought to warn you to keep your gratitude until you've arrived at your destination. Anything could happen between here and Birmingham when you travel with me,' he said.

She realised he was making an oblique reference to the accident for which he had been responsible and which had caused severe injury to his ex-girl-friend. Leaning forward impulsively, she placed a hand on his arm. Immediately he covered her hand with one of his.

'It's a chance I'm willing to take,' she said sincerely. 'I do trust you and I'm sure you won't let me down.'

'I'll do my best not to let you down,' he replied huskily, and a dull red colour stained his face. 'Thanks for trusting me, Gina. Now I'd better go and see to those dinghies for Will.'

Will did not come back in time for lunch, so there were only Gina, Irma and Gregor at the table for the midday meal. When it was over Irma said she would go and pack in readiness to leave as soon as Will put in an appearance.

'I hope he comes soon,' she said. 'I must leave at two o'clock and I do not want to leave without saying good-bye to him.'

'I'm sure he'll be back in time,' soothed Gina. 'Have you by any chance seen Blue this morning?'

'I think I saw him wandering off towards the cliffs,' replied Irma vaguely, as she left the kitchen.

Hoping that her pet would turn up soon, Gina went into the living room and tried to compose a letter to Will. The words would not flow and after several attempts which all found their way to the waste basket she wrote only:

Dear Will,
    Gregor has taken me to Birmingham. Thank you for having me.

She signed it simply with the name George and left it lying on the open desk. It didn't express at all her feelings about her stay in Glengorm, but she daren't write any more in case her emotions got the better of her. She recalled her first night at the White Lodge when Will had found the note from Gavin and felt suddenly guilty as if she were in the process of letting Will down too, and Meg Maxwell had warned that Will must not be let down again.

Shaking the feeling off, she left the room quickly before she could change her mind about the terse little note. She went upstairs, put on her red raincoat, picked up her cases, gave a last look round the room where she had slept so well for many nights, and then crept downstairs and out of the house. She hoped that Irma was too busy with her own packing to hear or notice anything unusual.

Outside she found Gregor leaning against Andrea's two-seater sports car, obviously ready to set off. He took the cases from her and put them in the space behind the seats where his own zipped holdall was already in position.

'I can't find Blue,' said Gina. 'Irma says she saw him going off towards the cliffs. I'll have to go and look for him.'

'I'll come with you,' offered Gregor, noting how white her face was and how wide and strained-looking her eyes were.

The smirr of rain had increased to a steady drenching downpour and by the time they reached the cliff top they were both soaked. Gina's bright hair was dark with rain and Gregor's hung in rat's tails over the collar of his short waterproof jacket.

157

There was no sign of the kitten and Gina went cautiously to the edge of the cliff to peer over down to the tossing, foaming water.

'Once he climbed down to a ledge and Will had to rescue him,' she explained to Gregor, and then she began to call the kitten.

Gregor shivered slightly as he also looked down the severe slope of the slippery shining rock.

'He could be anywhere,' he muttered. Then he grabbed her arm and added, 'Shush! Listen, I think I heard him crying.'

Gina stopped calling and listened intently. Below the sea crashed incessantly against the rocks at the foot of the cliffs. A solitary seagull glided by on a current of air, its screeching call seeming like a mocking echo of a cat's meow.

'It was the gull you heard,' she said miserably.

'No,' he insisted. 'Look—there's the kitten, down there, on that little ledge.'

She looked. Today there was no sunshine to make the rock flash with pink sparks. Instead it was dark grey with tiny rivulets of water streaming down it. About twenty feet below on a narrow ledge of rock which jutted out, something moved.

'Blue!' she called, and there was the unmistakable plaintive howl of a cat in trouble.

'He is there,' she exclaimed. 'Oh, the silly little thing! Why did he go down there just when I want to leave? What shall I do?'

'Keep on calling him. If he was able to get down there he should be able to get up. Cats rarely go to places from which they can't return,' suggested Gregor.

'But I've no time to wait for him. I must leave before Will comes back and Irma leaves,' moaned Gina desperately, seeing all her plans to help Irma and Will find happiness together disintegrating just because her kitten was too adventurous.

'Then you'll have to leave without him,' replied Gregor,

impatiently. 'He isn't all that important, surely?'

'Yes, he is. Oliver gave him to me,' said Gina, then realised suddenly, as she noticed puzzlement flash across Gregor's face, that he didn't know anything about Oliver and had never heard of him. 'I can't go without him. You must realise that,' she insisted. 'I'll have to stay and wait for him after all.'

He gave her a strange glance and then looked over the edge of the cliff again.

'If Will could climb down there I can,' he said with a touch of arrogance, and before she could remonstrate he had lowered himself over the edge of the cliff and was searching with his feet for suitable footholds while he clung to the edge with his hands.

'Oh, please be careful, Greg. It's very wet and slippery,' Gina urged anxiously, wondering what Mrs Macneal would say if she knew her youngest son was risking life and limb to fetch a silly little kitten from its precarious perch on the face of a cliff to safety, just because an equally silly young woman could not bear to go away without it. 'Perhaps you should get a rope first,' she added, as an afterthought.

He looked up at her his dark eyes glittering with some undefinable emotion.

'If we want to get away before Will comes back from Ullapool and Irma leaves, there isn't time for me to fetch a rope,' he retorted. 'Did Will use a rope?'

'No. But it was a fine day and he's much more . . .'

'I know,' he interrupted fiercely. 'He's much more experienced than I am in more ways than one, but he's not going to have you, if I can help it. If he didn't need a rope then neither do I. I'll show you that I'm as good as he is any day.'

Realising the futility of arguing with him when he was in such a strange stubborn mood, Gina walked away from the edge of the cliff, unable to stay and watch him climb down. She hoped he knew what he was doing, and began to wish she had agreed to leave the glen without the kitten.

After pacing up and down several times and succeeding only in soaking her feet in the wet grass, she gathered up enough nerve to go back and look over the edge again. To her relief Gregor was near the ledge. Leaning against the face of the cliff, he was reaching sideways with one hand to grasp the kitten. Spitting and snarling, Blue backed off, just out of reach.

'Oh, you stupid cat!' wailed Gina. She knelt on the wet grass, regardless of the damp patches such an action would leave on the knees of her elegant wheat-coloured pants. 'Can't you see that someone has come to rescue you?'

Watching tensely, she saw Gregor reach sideways again and fail to grasp the ball of wet, greyish-blue fur which was Blue. Then to her horror she saw him slip. He clutched desperately with his fingers to the wet rock as he tried to find new footholds, but without spikes on the soles of his shoes he was unable to get an adequate grip on the slippery surface. Slowly he began to slide down the cliff in the direction of the pounding, smashing sea.

CHAPTER SIX

PETRIFIED, her hands to her face, Gina knelt in the grass and watched Gregor's body gain momentum and begin to roll over and over down the cliff. Suddenly, with an unpleasant jolt, he came to a stop, his fall broken by a clump of bushes which grew out of a crevice in the rock. The branches of the bushes shook in reaction to the jolt and Gina prayed that they would hold him.

He lay still and she wondered if he had lost consciousness. She called to him, but her voice came out as a croak which the hovering seagull mimicked as it swooped down the cliff face, a flash of white against the dark grey.

Clearing her throat, she cupped her hands round her mouth and called again.

'Gregor, can you hear me?'

The kitten mewed plaintively and the seagull chattered mockingly. Gregor lifted an arm and waved it and Gina thought he called to her.

'Stay there!' she shouted. 'I'll go and fetch help.'

He waved again as if to acknowledge that he had heard her. She stood up and began to run down the path to White Lodge. The skirts of her raincoat caught at her legs and the wet grass seemed to suck her feet down, impeding her progress. As she ran she said over and over to herself, 'Please let Will be back from Ullapool. Please let Will be back.' Then she told herself not to waste her breath.

Panting for breath, she slithered down the last slippery stretch of the path to the house. With relief she saw that the blue truck was parked in its usual place near the barn.

'Will, Will,' she started to shout breathlessly, 'where are you?'

He could be anywhere on the estate, she realised. On the other side of the loch, on the moors, in the barn. Or he could be with Irma in the house.

Frantically she flung herself at the front door, opening it and almost falling into the hallway.

'Will!' she called.

He came out of the living room almost immediately. She had a brief impression that he was rather pale and that the expression in his eyes was one of cold wicked anger. Then she was in his arms and gasping out her story about Gregor.

'Now, George, this is no way to behave when someone needs help.' His voice was calm, as reassuring as ever. His hands were on her shoulders, holding her away from him. When she looked up she saw he was no longer pale and his eyes, though cold, did not flicker with that livid violent emotion.

'Pull yourself together,' he ordered crisply, 'and tell me slowly what happened exactly, when he slipped and where he is now, while we go and choose some ropes from the storage shed. Then you'll have to go and tell Lachie that I'll need his help.'

He turned and opened the front door and pushed her before him, out into the damp drizzle.

'And Irma too,' she suggested. 'She's strong, and could help.'

'Irma has gone. She left about ten minutes ago,' he replied curtly, as he strode ahead of her towards the bunk-houses.

Looking round, Gina realised that the grey Volkswagen was no longer parked beside the two-seater which belonged to Andrea Macneal. Her plan to leave before Irma had mis-fired after all. Irma had gone. Was it possible that her de-parture was the reason why Will had looked so pale and angry when he had come out of the living room?

As she caught up with him she described once again, as clearly as she could, what had happened to Gregor. By the time she had finished they had reached the storage shed, where only a few hours earlier she had made plans to leave the glen, and Will was selecting lengths of terylene rope.

He gave her a sidelong glance, said something vitriolic and unkind about Blue, then, when she would have retaliated in defence of her pet, smiled at her in a way which made her heart lurch suddenly and pink colour storm into her cheeks, and added gently,

'You're all of a dither, aren't you, love? Don't worry, I'll rescue Greg for you and bring him up all in one piece. Now go and tell Lachie to come here. Then take Andrea's car ...'

'No keys,' she interrupted him. 'Greg has them in his pocket.'

'Then take the truck.' He dropped the keys into her outstretched hand. 'Go to Castle Duich and tell Mrs Macneal, or whoever is there, what's happened. Say you need the help of some strong men, preferably some with climbing knowledge. Grant Parker and a couple of the shepherds would do. Ask for arrangements to be made for Greg to be taken to hospital as soon as he's brought up. He may have broken ribs or limbs after a fall like that. Now, hurry!'

'I don't know the way to the castle,' she gasped, thinking how much better she felt now that he had taken charge.

'Go to Lochinvie, right through the village and take the first road to the left. The castle is signposted and you can't miss the way.'

'Thank you. You'll be careful, Will, please,' she begged earnestly. 'The rock is awfully slippery. I wouldn't like you to fall too.'

His clear cold eyes appraised her and he lifted an eyebrow in sardonic appreciation of her remark.

'Nice of you to care, George,' he drawled drily. 'Unlike Greg, I shan't take any unnecessary risks, not even for you. Now off you go to Lachie's cottage.'

He turned his back on her. She hesitated a moment, gazing in puzzlement at his broad shoulders. Once again she realised how little she knew about him; about his real feelings. She could only guess that something had happened to upset him, and her guess was that he was regretting Irma's departure.

Leaving the shed, she walked down to Lachie's cottage. She found him in his kitchen sitting in front of a peat fire, smoking his pipe and reading the newspaper. Lachie did not like to work on a wet day. He listened to her carefully and courteously, then without a word, he stood up, took down an old oilskin coat from the hook behind the door, put it on, clapped a disreputable tweed hat on his head, ushered here out of the cottage, and strode away in the direction of the bunkhouses.

Gina hurried after him and went straight to the truck. After a few false starts she managed to get it going and guided it gingerly along the narrow road through the glen, lurching and bumping over potholes, brimful of muddy water.

Lochinvie was a single deserted street of squat thatched cottages. Thin spirals of smoke rose from the chimneys adding to the grey cloud which hovered over the whole area. Beyond the cottages Gina found the road to the left and turned on to it, thankful to see that it was surfaced and in good repair so that she was able to accelerate.

After twenty minutes of driving round innumerable bends as the road wound, a dark grey ribbon of wet tarmac across dank dismal moorland which stretched drearily for miles under heavy purplish-grey clouds, Gina was glad when she saw a signpost which indicated that Castle Duich was only half a mile away.

At last the road straightened, cutting through a forest of gloomy dripping-wet spruce trees. Imposing stone gateposts appeared on the left and she turned the truck to drive between them up a wide driveway which led to a massive pile of stone masonry. Turrets and battlements reared up against the cloudy sky, giving the castle an authentic Gothic appearance and bringing to mind stories of vampires and ghosts. The yellow gleam of electric light glowed here and there from latticed windows, deep-set in the thick walls.

Gina parked the truck and jumped down. She ran to the

great oak door which was under a curved archway. She pulled on the old-fashioned doorbell handle and was relieved when the door swung open silently to reveal a tall man. Judging by his green suit, which was fastened by large brass buttons, he was some sort of servant, although the glance he gave her down his nose was extremely supercilious, as if he considered she had no right to approach the castle by the front entrance.

She explained why she was there. Without hesitation he invited her into a wide hall which had a stone floor. Ancient banners hung from authentic smoke-blackened beams. Colourful woven tapestries depicting hunting scenes decorated the thick stone walls. Light from wrought iron chandeliers glinted on shields and heraldic crests, which decorated the stone canopy of the huge fireplace.

The footman told her to sit on one of the high-backed Jacobean oak chairs which lined the walls, and went off to find Mrs Macneal. Sitting on the edge of the chair her hands in her pockets, Gina gazed around in awe at her surroundings and wondered how she was going to explain to Mrs Macneal that her youngest son was lying in a precarious position half way down a cliff.

In a very short time the click of a woman's high heels on stone flooring announced the coming of Mrs Macneal. She came through an archway on the right, small and imperious, wearing her magnificent kilt with a plain black woollen sweater.

Her dark brown eyes took in Gina's wet dishevelled hair and mud-stained raincoat in one comprehensive glance before she started to speak.

'Where is Gregor?' she rapped.

The words tumbled out of Gina as she explained. As when telling Will about the accident she left out the part that she and Gregor had been about to set off for Birmingham together, thinking that it would only cause Mrs Macneal to ask more questions.

'It's all my fault,' she ended in a low voice. 'I shouldn't

have let him climb down the cliff. He might be seriously hurt or even...' She caught her breath shakily, unable to say the word *dead*.

The austere lines of Mrs Macneal's patrician face softened slightly and she sat down on the chair next to Gina.

'You mustn't blame yourself, my dear,' she soothed, the pride of generations of Macneals preventing her from showing any extreme emotion on hearing that her son might be badly hurt. 'He *chose* to go for your kitten and I'm pleased that he felt he wanted to help someone at a risk to himself. There was a time, you know, when he would not have lifted a finger to help anyone, but you've changed all that.'

'I?' exclaimed Gina, raising surprised golden eyes to the imperious fine-featured face of the chief of the Macneals. 'What have I done?'

'You have been here in the right place at the right time,' insisted Mrs Macneal. 'When he met you Gregor was rudderless, incapable of steering in any direction for more than a few hours at a time. In order to impress you he has made an effort to come to terms with himself. I'm grateful to you, Gina, for giving him help when he needed it most, and I'd like to think that you'll always be his friend. I wish you could be more, but unfortunately Will Fox stands in the way of that wish coming true, just as he stands in the way of a few of my wishes. Now I'm going to take you to Andrea and she'll see that you have some tea while I go and arrange for some men to go over and help Will to rescue Gregor.'

From then on everything happened so quickly that Gina was slightly bewildered. Andrea appeared and took her off to a pleasant sitting room where a young man was lounging before a fire listening to a record player. Andrea introducd him as Blake Fraser, her cousin from the States, and then bombarded her with questions about Gregor's fall. They were just drinking tea when Mrs Macneal walked into the room. She was dressed in a white riding mackintosh and wore a coloured headscarf over her hair.

'I'm going over to the cliff now,' she announced. 'Everything is arranged. An ambulance will be sent to White Lodge immediately.'

'I hope it can get through,' said Gina. 'The glen road is like a river.'

'Then it's high time the County Council did something about it,' snapped Mrs Macneal, every inch the chieftain. She had probably never given a thought to the road, which she had hardly ever used, until today, when it was essential that access to the glen should be as easy as possible so that her youngest son could be transported to hospital. 'There should be a decent road now that there's someone living permanently at White Lodge. I'll take the matter up with the Council personally.'

She swept out of the room, leaving Gina to the tender mercies of Andrea, who talked almost vivaciously about the show-jumping competitions in which she had participated over the years. The vivacity was put on, Gina realised, for the benefit of the laconic Blake, and not for her. As soon as she could, she excused herself saying she must go back to White Lodge to find out what was happening. To her surprise Andrea said she would go with her in order to bring back her car, and soon Gina was driving back across the moors with Andrea sitting beside her.

The rain had stopped temporarily and the mist-like clouds had rolled up to reveal the severe rocky ramparts of the mountains which they had been hiding most of the day. Watery sunlight shone for a few minutes, striking diamond-like flashes of light from the wet trunks of trees and from the glistening dry-stone walls.

Inside the cab of the truck Andrea was silent, obviously ill at ease now that she was alone with Gina. The vivacity had been left behind at the castle along with the American cousin. It was not until they had begun to descend towards Lochinvie that she found her tongue. Then she spoke roughly and jerkily.

'Greg's in love with you,' she announced.

167

Gina gripped the steering wheel hard and kept her glance directed at the stretch of road in front of her.

'I don't think so,' she replied coolly.

'Then why has he spent so much time at White Lodge recently?' challenged Andrea.

'He wanted to prove that he could do something positive, and he has,' replied Gina firmly.

'By falling down a cliff?' Andrea was scornful. 'If the kitten hadn't been yours he wouldn't have gone after it. He's in love with you,' she asserted. 'You must be feeling very pleased with yourself. You stole Will away from me, and as if that wasn't enough, you have my brother dangling after you and climbing down cliffs for you, behaving like a knight in some chivalrous romance, doing dangerous deeds just to please his lady.'

Gina gritted her teeth. She must not allow herself to be upset by anything Andrea said, reminding herself that every word the girl uttered was the product of sour grapes. On the other hand she decided that it was time Miss Andrea Macneal learnt the truth.

'That is untrue,' she said coolly. 'In the first place I couldn't steal Will from you because he wasn't and never has been yours to steal. He regards you as a schoolgirl, and any feeling that you have for him he sees as mere infactuation, which he can do without because he finds it embarrassing.'

She heard Andrea draw in her breath sharply as if in pain and realised ruefully that she would have to pay for making that remark. Andrea was too spiteful to let it pass unpunished.

'And in the second place,' she continued, 'Gregor and I are good friends, nothing more. He's not in love with me.'

Unfortunately her voice faltered a little as she made the statement about Gregor. She had just recalled the ardent glow in his eyes that morning when he had heard she was about to jilt Will. He could not and must not be in love with her, she thought rather wildly, because she was certainly not in love with him. She found him attractive and good company, but she was not in love with him or anyone else. She wasn't even in love with Oliver any more.

But Andrea had noticed the quaver in her voice and with her usual quickness she pounced at once.

'You don't sound very sure,' she sneered. 'You needn't keep up appearances with me, you know. I expect you're sorry that you're engaged to Will now that you've met Gregor. Perhaps you'd like to jilt Will? Why don't you? Why don't you give him back his diamond ring and marry Gregor instead? I can assure you you'd please my mother if you did. She thinks you're the best person to ever cross my playboy brother's path, so you wouldn't find any opposition there.'

'And I suppose if I did jilt him you'll be ready and waiting to comfort Will?' retorted Gina tartly. 'Catch him on the rebound—is that your little plan? Yes, I can imagine that's the only way you could get him.'

Again Andrea drew a sharp breath and again Gina wished she had said nothing.

'Yes, I would like to comfort him,' said Andrea. 'And if you like I'll tell him for you that you're in love with Gregor and that he loves you. Then Will can do the right thing by you and release you from your engagement to save you from jilting him. Of course, you must realise that it's possible he knows you've been two-timing him during the past few weeks ever since you met Gregor!'

Gina seethed in silence. There was little use in denying Andrea's accusation and telling her that it was impossible for Will to be two-timed by herself when she was not properly engaged to him. To do so would involve her in a long explanation which she was not free to make, for the simple reason that their 'engagement' was Will's secret as well as her own, and he had used it to protect himself against gossip as well as from Andrea and her mother.

Fortunately Andrea accepted her silence as a sign of defeat and made no more scathing comments or suggestions, so the rest of the journey was made without a word being said by either of them.

They reached the white house amongst the birches just as rain began to fall again. There was a big ambulance parked close to the path coming down from the cliffs, and its rear doors were open ready to receive a stretcher. Two other vehicles were parked in front of the house—Mrs Macneal's Rolls-Royce, and a Land-Rover with the words Castle Duich painted on its dark green door.

Gina was about to start walking up the path, with Andrea close behind her, when she saw a group of people coming towards her. With a word to Andrea she turned back and they both stood and waited beside the ambulance.

Mrs Macneal headed the procession. With her hands at the pockets of her riding mackintosh and her headscarf soaked with rain she still managed to look regal and self-confident. Behind her came the stretcher to which Gregor had been bound. It was carried by the two ambulance men and was followed by two other men, both wearing dark green tweed suits, obviously the gamekeepers from the Castle Duich estate.

'Is he badly hurt?' asked Gina urgently, looking down at Gregor's white face which was blotched with purple bruises. His eyes had been closed, but when he heard her voice he opened them and they looked like dark empty caverns in his pale face.

'One broken leg. Could have been worse,' said Mrs Macneal brusquely.

'Oh, Gregor, I'm terribly sorry. It was my fault. I should have gone without the kitten,' said Gina softly, walking along beside the stretcher.

He smiled faintly, a ghost of his attractive flashing smile.

'Not your fault,' he murmured, with some difficulty because the pain-killer which the ambulance men had given him was beginning to take effect and make him drowsy. 'I wanted to show you that I'm as good as Will. At least I thought I was as good as him. I'm nothing but a show-off. I

170

always have been. Next time I'll do as he says. I'll think first and act afterwards.'

He was being lifted into the ambulance and he raised his head a little so that he could still see her.

'Thank Will and Lachie for coming to the rescue, please, Gina. Come and see me in hospital. You mustn't leave the glen. You mustn't go to Birmingham. You must stay.' He sounded suddenly desperate. 'Mother, tell her, please. She's not to go away.'

His voice faded as he disappeared into the ambulance. Mrs Macneal entered the vehicle and Gina could hear her saying something to him. Then the rear doors were closed, the ambulance men took their seats in front and the heavy vehicle lumbered away along the road.

Gina and Andrea stood side by side and watched it go.

'I suppose I'd better go to the hospital too. Mother seems to expect it,' muttered Andrea sulkily, having looked around and made sure that Will was nowhere about. 'Do you want to come with me?'

'No, thank you,' replied Gina, who was determined to do nothing which would make Andrea think she was interested in Gregor.

The girl glanced past her up the path, but no one was coming from the cliff, so with a shrug of her shoulders she turned away and went off to the two-seater car.

Soon the car was leaving with a roar of exhaust, closely followed by the Land-Rover. Gina watched them go and then turned to the path, intending to find Will and Lachie.

She did not have to go far. They were strolling towards her, ropes coiled over their shoulders, moving in a leisurely fashion in spite of the rain, as if they had all day. At the sight of Will's damp tousled hair and his wide shoulders under the old green Army sweater he was wearing, Gina felt a sudden lift of relief mingled with delight. He had dared danger to rescue Gregor and he had succeeded in his usual calm competent way.

As he came nearer she saw that he had also rescued Blue,

for he was carrying the wet and miserable kitten between his hands. He came right up to her and held the cat out to her.

'This is yours, I believe. I'm surprised to find you here. I thought you'd be away in the ambulance holding Greg's hand,' he remarked drily.

She took the kitten from him and held it close to her. A little hurt by his taunt about Gregor, she gazed at Will, her eyes wide and troubled. She noticed that the rain had made his hair curl more closely to his head; that the skin was taut across his cheekbones and round his jaw, emphasising the strong clean angles of his face; that his eyes were as cold and clear as the water in a burn; and that the curve to his mouth was sardonic as he returned her gaze. Once before, in her parents' home, he had shown disapproval of her and now she could *feel* that same disapproval travelling like an electric current from him to her. She had done something which he disliked and for the time being he hated her.

'I'll be on my way,' Lachie was muttering, as if he sensed there was trouble brewing between them and he wished to be gone before it broke. 'That was a fine piece of rescue work you and I were doing on the cliff there, Will. Not that Macneal's men weren't a help, they were, but without you and me they wouldn't have known where to start. And I'm thinking yon kitten has nine lives, so it has.'

He went off, and in the silence he left behind him Gina could hear rain pattering on the leaves of the rhododendron bushes, on the roof of the porch and on the stiff shiny material of her red raincoat.

Will started off towards the house. She fell into step beside him.

'Gregor asked me to thank you for rescuing him,' she said hurriedly.

'Why haven't you gone to the hospital with him?' he asked coolly, ignoring her thanks.

'I was afraid Mrs Macneal might misunderstand if I did,' she replied.

He raised that infuriating eyebrow at her, making her feel as if she had spoken illogically.

'Really?' he remarked with a touch of irony. 'You shouldn't worry about that. She thinks very highly of you. She keeps telling me that you're far too good for a bawdy-minded ex-soldier like me. She seems to think that in time I'll believe that she's right and I'll break off our engagement so that her beloved Gregor can try his chances with you. I gather she doesn't know you were about to elope with him.'

'We weren't eloping,' she stormed at him, eyes blazing with green-gold fire as her anger was roused by his sardonic needling. Then suddenly remembering she gasped, 'Oh, you found my note!'

'Yes, I found your note. You intended that I should find it, didn't you?' he jeered. 'I seem to go through life finding notes left by people who walk out on me as if they're afraid to tell me the truth. Gregor's accident seems to have put paid to your plans, so what are you going to do now?'

Gina licked her lips which were suddenly dry. Surely he wouldn't turn her away from his house just because she had intended to leave with Gregor instead of waiting for him to take her. She searched his face for some signs of mockery, but it was quite hard and his eyes were still cold.

'I thought I could——' she began, then changed her mind. 'Please could you let me stay another night?' she asked in a small voice. 'And please could you take me south tomorrow as you promised?'

He regarded her narrowly, his mouth twisting unpleasantly.

'You can stay the night,' he agreed curtly, 'but I'm not making any promises about tomorrow. That's another day and anything could happen between now and then.'

Gina felt fear prickle her skin. Threat underlined his words. He was going to make her pay somehow for attempting to leave without telling him.

He thrust open the door.

'Go in,' he ordered brusquely, 'and feed your damned cat. I'll go and dump these ropes and when I come back you and I are going to have a straight talk.'

Gina went into the house quickly and the door closed behind her. In the hall she set Blue down, took off her raincoat, kicked off her shoes and went into the kitchen to find milk and food for the kitten. All the time her mind was busy searching for ways to placate Will when he came in so that he wouldn't punish her too severely.

He would be wet, as she was, and he would be tired after the physical and mental effort of organising Gregor's rescue. He would want hot water to wash in and something hot to drink. She would change out of her damp clothes and then make some tea.

Her thoughts skidded to a stop. All her clothes were in her cases which were in Andrea's car. She would have to make do with towelling her hair and making it tidy.

While she was combing her hair she heard Will enter the house. He was whistling, a sound which made her relax a little. He wouldn't whistle if he were still in a bad mood. He bypassed the kitchen and went upstairs, and soon she could hear the sound of water running in the bathroom.

When he came to the kitchen she would attack first, she decided. She would ask him why he had let Irma go. She was sure that the departure of the German woman was the cause of his dourness. Then, when she had the advantage, she would tell him the real reason for her decision to leave the glen before Irma left.

Footsteps on the stairs warned her of his approach. She made the tea and set the pot on the table, turning to greet him with a smile.

'Why haven't you changed out of those damp clothes?' he rapped, and immediately her advantage was lost before she had even opened her mouth.

'All my clothes are in Andrea's car,' she explained.

'So you were eloping,' he accused.

His hair was still damp and ruffled. The taut skin across

174

his cheekbones was aglow from exposure to the rain that afternoon. He had changed into a blue shirt which she had not seen before, and he was still in the process of buttoning it down the front, so that she had a brief tantalising glimpse of his white-skinned muscular chest, blurred by dark hair.

He was different, or so she thought, not realising that the difference was in herself, changing her view of him. He was no longer just Oliver's rather unconventional elder brother, who had been concerned about her and had wanted to help her. He was a vigorous, powerful man with whom she had lived for almost six weeks and who had once held her in his arms and had asked her to take the next step with him. He was Will, dear and familiar to her; someone she could love with all her body and soul.

'Come on, George, stop day-dreaming!' his voice seemed to come from a long way off, rallying her, tormenting her. 'Admit that you and Gregor were running away together.'

'But we weren't,' she retorted. 'I asked him to take me to the nearest train going south and he offered to drive me all the way to Birmingham.'

'For nothing?' he gibed. 'I can't imagine young Gregor not wanting payment of some sort. Why couldn't you wait for me to take you?'

'Because I thought it might help you and Irma if I left before she did,' she quavered, watching one muscular forearm appear as he turned up the long sleeve of his shirt in neat Army-like folds, noticing how the hair-blurred skin rippled and ridged as he clenched his fist. Strange how she was noticing far more about his physical appearance than she had ever noticed before. It was as though she had come alive and was seeing properly for the first time since she had met him.

'And what little romance have you been weaving about Irma and me?' he asked dryly, as he started to roll up the other sleeve.

'I thought that once I'd left you'd be able to tell her that

175

you weren't engaged to me any more, and then—and then . . .'

His eyes had begun to dance with mockery, their colour changing to a darker, warmer blue, making her forget what she had been going to say next.

'Go on, George. This is most interesting,' he urged, coming to stand close to her. The thin stuff of his shirt was taut across his shoulders and his chest emphasising their muscularity. In the hollow below the strong column of his throat she could see a pulse beating regularly. He smelt of spicy soap and she found his powerful, vibrant virility almost overwhelming. It made her feel slightly groggy and she wished wildly that he would move away.

'When I told Irma that you and I weren't engaged any more what was supposed to happen then?' he prompted scoffingly.

'You could have asked her to marry you. I know she's very fond of you. She told me so herself, and I think you're fond of her,' she stammered, her glance meeting his only briefly before sliding away from that amused twinkle in his eyes.

'You believe that fondness is sufficient basis for marriage?' he probed.

She didn't answer because she was experiencing strong desire to fling her arms around him and to stop his mocking taunts with kisses, letting such an embrace lead her willy-nilly to the next step.

'No answer?' he jeered. 'Then let me answer for you. It isn't. I've no wish to marry Irma, nor has she any wish to marry me. In fact I think she might marry a very good friend of mine who's still in the Army.'

Gina looked up then, her eyes wide and startled.

'Then what was she doing here?' she demanded, feeling very foolish and naïve.

'Just visiting, as she said. She was on holiday and while she was in Britain she thought she'd look me up and bring me news of people I used to know in Hamburg. She didn't

176

intend to stay, but you invited her to, and I must admit she was a great help while the campers were here.'

'Oh.' Gina felt deflated. 'But she told me she was staying to make sure you didn't make the same mistake twice. She thought I was like Bridget and that you'd been attracted by the same type of woman.'

'If it's any consolation to you, George,' he said gently, 'I can tell you that she'd decided by the end of her stay here that you aren't as soft and helpless as you appear. Now let's get back to you and Gregor. Have you told him we're not engaged?'

'I told him that I was going to jilt you so that you could marry Irma. Oh, what a mess! Another mess! I thought I was helping you and Irma and all I've done is cause Gregor to be hurt badly,' she moaned.

'Never mind,' he comforted. 'It was his own decision to go after Blue, and he recognises that. He's come a long way in these past weeks. Why don't you stay a little longer so that you can visit him while his leg is mending? Now that you've jilted me you needn't worry how it will look,' he suggested.

He was her kind friend again, trying to help her by making it easy for her to visit Gregor because he thought that was what she wanted to do most. His kindness, however, was hurting much more than his unkindness had, and she pushed it away.

'No, thank you. You'll have to take me to that train to-morrow,' she said. 'It's time I left, Will. You've been very kind and helpful, but I'm better now. I can face up to life again without any help.'

Her voice shook and she had to turn away quickly. Then his hands were on her shoulders and sliding forward over her breast so that she was pulled against him. Held like that against his warm body she was a prisoner who had no wish to escape. She felt his cheek against her hair. He whispered in her ear,

'I'll miss *you*, when you've gone, not just your cooking,'

Gina closed her eyes and held her breath as she searched for the right words to say before the magic of the moment was lost; words which would lead her to the next step.

The front door opened and closed. Andrea's deep husky voice called Gina's name and brought the search to an abrupt end. Will released her suddenly and she went rather blindly from the kitchen into the hall.

Andrea's dark eyes were bright and inquisitive as she looked past Gina to Will and then back again to Gina.

'I've brought your cases,' she said. 'I thought you might need them.'

'I'll go and fetch them in,' murmured Will, passing Gina and going out of the house.

'I thought you'd like to know too, that Gregor's leg is broken only in one place and that he should be up on crutches soon,' said Andrea. 'He told me to tell you he'd like you to visit him, and Mother said I was to tell you that you'll be welcome at the castle any time.'

'I'm afraid that won't be possible,' replied Gina stiffly. 'I'm going to Birmingham tomorrow. My home is there, you know, and I'm not married to Will yet. Gregor was just being helpful by taking me down there instead of Will.'

'I see,' drawled Andrea, her disbelief showing in her arched eyebrows. 'In that case I'll say good-bye, and hope that you'll never come back.'

She turned on her heel and went out of the house back to the car. Gina paused long enough to watch her talking to Will, then she went back into the kitchen to drink cold tea. Eventually Will came into the house and she heard him go upstairs with her cases as the sports car roared away. When he came downstairs again he put his head round the kitchen door to announce gruffly that it was time he did some work on the farm, then left the house again, banging the front door behind him.

She did not see him again until he came in for the evening meal, and then he was uncommunicative, the expression in his eyes distant. When she spoke to him he answered

178

absently and in the end she withdrew into silence herself, hurt by his withdrawal.

Evening sunlight, breaking through the clouds, slanted into the room and Gina wondered where she would be the same time the next day. Still travelling south, she supposed, her back turned on Glengorm and all that it had offered.

Her throat grew tight and the room blurred before her eyes. Excusing herself from the table, she began to collect dishes in readiness for washing up. Through the window above the sink she could see the swans swimming on the loch, taking advantage of the evening sunshine after a day of rain. Later she would go and feed them.

She heard Will leave the kitchen. A few moments later he came back with Lachie.

'I was just passing the door and it came to my mind that I should be telling you what I was doing this morning in the town,' Lachie was explaining in his sing-song voice.

'Sit down and tell me, then,' replied Will easily, going over to the cupboard where he kept his whisky. 'Would you take a dram while you're talking?'

'Aye, I will,' sighed Lachie, settling into one of the chairs at the table. 'I've been feeling a wee bit chilly this evening. We were after getting awful wet this afternoon. A wee dram would be fine, that is if you're taking one yourself?'

He would be there for the rest of the evening, thought Gina, with a sinking heart. His voice would drone on and on like the bagpipes. Will, patient and forbearing with him, would sit there listening to tales he must have heard many times. Occasionally he would say a few words, but it would be Lachie who would hold the floor. Then when the older man had taken his fill of whisky he would decide it was time he went to bed and would leave. Even his leave-taking would be a long-drawn-out affair because he would linger on the doorstep, talking about the stars, if there were any to see, or the weather forecast, and always he would 'mind' a

179

day when something or other had happened and off his drone would start again.

She supposed he would be here tomorrow evening, and every evening after that. In her mind the evenings stretched into weeks, months, years, with Will sitting there listening to Lachie, until *his* dark hair began to turn grey, *his* broad straight shoulders began to stoop a little and he lost his gaiety and enthusiasm and became just another elderly man, alone and lonely in the glen with only memories for company.

Tears dimmed her eyes again as she finished drying the last dish. Lachie could have stayed away for this last evening with Will, the first time they had been alone together without the ghosts of Bridget and Oliver standing between them.

She put the dishes away and wiped down the draining board. Already the two men were on their second dram of whisky and Lachie's voice was chanting away.

'Well now,' he was saying, 'I'm going to tell you what has been in my mind these past six weeks. You'll be knowing Flora Kennedy who works as housekeeper at Castle Duich?'

Will murmured that he did know the woman.

'A fine woman, so she is. I've been knowing her all my life,' said Lachie. 'We went to school together. She buried her husband five years ago. Ach, he was a fine fisherman, was Angus. I mind the day when he and I were fishing the Gorm Water.'

Lachie was off on a tangent, reminiscing for all he was worth. Heaven only knew when he would tell them what had been on his mind for these last six weeks concerning Flora Kennedy.

Taking a bag of bread she had saved for the swans, Gina slipped out of the room, unhooked her raincoat from the peg in the hallway put it on and stepped out of the house.

Crimson-tinted bars of cloud streaked the primrose-coloured sky in the west as the sun slid below the horizon, and

180

the glen was full of green and blue shadow. In the twilight the birches were silvery ghosts as she passed through them and the smell of damp earth tangled with the smell of the sea.

At her approach the swans swam over to the beach, and because Blue wasn't with her, they waddled ashore and came close to take bread from her fingers with their orange and black beaks.

When the swans return to Glengorm the curse will be lifted and the true mistress of the master of the glen will come back. Until that time the glen will not hold a woman.

That was the curse associated with the long absence of the swans from the glen, and Lachie had thought it had been lifted when the two swans had flown into the glen one day in April and she had come with Will, wearing an engagement ring on her left hand.

But she wasn't Will's true mistress. She was only his pseudo-fiancée and tomorrow she would be going away. The swans would stay, so there was the possibility, if one believed in legends and curses, that another woman would come to the glen; someone who would be willing to take that further step with Will, the step he had asked her to take one evening in the lamplit dusk. It was possible some other woman would know his strength and his kindness, his roughness and his gentleness, and would learn to love him.

Gina shivered suddenly. Will had said that he would miss her. She would miss him too. She would miss his noisy banging on her bedroom door in the morning, his often caustic comments about her sleepiness, his whistling of a certain saucy song which told a story of slow seduction. Above all she would miss that dangerous delight which being alone with him in the quiet house brought to her.

She couldn't go. She would have to stay and take that next step with him no matter where it might lead. Maybe she would have to leave eventually, in September when the swans winged south again, but September was a long time ahead and the important time for Will and herself was now, while Mary was still painting the glen with the fresh greens and blues which gave it its name. Together they would watch the summer months bring their own deeper richer colours to the glen and see the offspring of the swans learn to swim and fly.

There was hope in her thoughts; hope for the future of the glen as well as for the future of herself and Will. Her mind suddenly crystal clear about her next move, Gina threw the last of the bread on the water. The swans waddled forward and slid silently into the loch. Swinging on her heel, she walked up the path through the ghostly birches to the house, and there was a lightness in her step which had not been there for many weeks.

Now her thoughts picked back over her relationship with Will. It had begun explosively and unconventionally in her bedroom at the flat. It had continued to be unconventional proceeding at an easy pace set by Will as he had nursed her back to normality, taunting her and then tempting her, he had coaxed her out of the protective cocoon she had spun round herself when Oliver had died. Now she was alive again, reborn and ready to love him if he would let her.

When she reachd the house she saw to her surprise that Lachie was leaving. He was loping down the road, singing to himself one of those long Gaelic ballads of which he was so fond. Forty-two verses and all of them the same, she had once heard Will jokingly describe the lilting songs.

She watched Lachie going, and smiled to herself, no longer resenting him. When Will was as old as the crofter he would have more to remember and, if luck was with her in the future, he would not sleep alone because she would be with him.

She entered the house quietly, and took off her raincoat. Creeping to the kitchen door, she looked into the room. Will was still sitting at the head of the table. He was shuffling a pack of playing cards and in the mellow glow of the lamp light his craggy face was all angles and shadows, difficult to read.

182

As she approached him he looked up briefly, a lightning flicker of pale blue eyes, and said curtly,

'I was just coming to look for you. I'd like you to do something for me.'

'What would you like me to do?' she asked, her voice slightly husky with excitement.

'Give up any idea of leaving here tomorrow and stay for the rest of the summer,' he said, still very curt.

He had asked her to do just what she had intended to do, but his manner of asking was so cool and crisp that she felt slightly rebuffed.

'Any particular reason?' she asked, trying to be cool and crisp too.

'Yes. Lachie is going to marry Flora Kennedy,' he replied concisely, as if that explained everything.

Slowly and deliberately he cut the pack of cards into two. Then picking up the two separate packs he mixed them together expertly, flicking them with his thumbs so that they made a clicking sound. That done, he selected the one from the top of the pack and laid it face upwards on the table. It was the ten of spades. Quickly he laid six other cards in a row besides the first one, their patterned backs showing upwards.

'But what has Lachie's plan to marry Flora Kennedy got to do with me staying for the rest of the summer?' she asked, feeling disappointed because he was not asking her to stay for a more personal reason.

He continued to set out the cards in rows, each row one card shorter than the row above it.

'He's wanted to marry her for years but hasn't dared to ask her because he believed in the curse. He was afraid to ask her to come and live in the glen in case she died suddenly as his first wife did,' he murmured, not lifting his glance from the cards.

'Couldn't they have gone to live elsewhere?' said Gina.

He shook his head slowly from side to side. He had finished setting out the cards and now he was picking up the ones which lay with their backs upwards, one by one.

'Not Lachie. He couldn't live anywhere else but Glengorm. He would always be hankering to come back here,' he replied. 'When the swans came back and you came to the glen with me he assumed that you and I were going to be married. Like Gregor, he saw Noll's ring on your finger and assumed it was mine. He's been waiting and watching ever since. Now he's decided that you're here to stay and that his problem is solved. He thinks the curse has been lifted so he's asked Flora to marry him. She's accepted his proposal and they'll be married three weeks from tomorrow. He came to tell me tonight. I hadn't the heart to tell him that you would be leaving tomorrow and would probably not return. I'm asking you to stay, George, please, for Lachie's sake, at least until they're married and Flora is settled in the glen.'

Her mind in a turmoil, Gina gazed at his big hands moving amongst the cards. Down by the loch everything had been clear. She had recognised that she could love him and live with him and she had come to tell him, expecting nothing in return except his rousing kisses, which would have led inevitably to the next step in their relationship. Now she was in a muddle again and wasn't at all sure whether he wanted her after all.

Suddenly she was reminded of the evening when he had stood and watched her working at her embroidery. Something of the irritation he must have felt then rose up within her as she watched him calmly picking up cards and laying them down in new positions. Apparently he was far more interested in the outcome of his game of Patience than he was in her.

Leaning forward, she snatched the few cards he was holding in one hand and flung them across the room, startling the kitten which was sleeping in its basket. Then with a sweeping movement of her hand she scattered the cards on the table in all directions.

For an electric moment green-shot golden eyes blazed

down into frost-blue eyes, which slowly darkened and began to dance with devilment.

'Well, well,' drawled Will softly, pushing back his chair and rising to his feet slowly. Coming round the corner of the table, he began to walk menacingly towards her, forcing her back against the wall. 'I wondered when you'd come alive. What caused that little display of temper?'

'You did!' she seethed. 'You're so smug, so confident that I'll stay. But why should I stay for Lachie's sake? Why don't you ask me to stay for your sake? Don't you ever want anything for yourself?'

'As a matter of fact, since you ask, I do want something for myself,' he replied tranquilly, standing over her, his brawny arms crossed over his chest. 'I want you, but only when you're ready, and not half alive.'

'Supposing,' she whispered shakily, putting a hand upon his forearm to caress it with her fingers, lifting her eyelids slowly to look up at him, feeling the blood rush to her face as for the first time in her life she made a deliberate attempt to entice a man, 'Supposing I told you that I'm ready now, what would you do?'

He left her in no doubt about what he would do. In a second she was in his arms and crushed against him. His kiss was all she had anticipated it would be and she responded readily to it, feeling desire scorch through her, its flame devouring any final doubts she might have had herself. When they drew apart at last they were both breathless.

'We'll have to be married,' Will murmured huskily into her hair. 'That's the next step for us.'

Once again he had surprised her. She had been sure that when he had originally asked her to take the next step with him marriage had not been his intention. She pulled away from him so that she could see his face. He returned her searching gaze steadily, an expression of such tenderness in his eyes that for a moment she wondered whether this was really her familiar rough and sometimes rude friend.

'You said once that you'd tried marriage and that it didn't work,' she exclaimed.

'I know I did. At the time I meant every word because I didn't want you or any other woman to get any ideas about tying me down,' he said with a touch of cynicism. 'It didn't work for Bridget and me and I vowed after she died that I'd never marry again. Brief affairs with no emotional involvement and no regrets at parting would be acceptable, but nothing permanent any more. That was how I had it all planned, and so it was, with a reasonable amount of success, until I fell in love with you.'

'Oh!' gasped Gina, highly diverted by this admission on his part. 'When did you fall in love with me?'

His teasing grin appeared. Pushing his hands into his trouser pockets, he rocked back and forth on his heels.

'I'm not sure. I was attracted to you from the first time I laid eyes on you in your bedroom at the flat, but I thought you were just another attractively packaged parcel, all show and no depth, soft and silken to the touch, but cold and empty underneath.'

'As Bridget was?' she whispered.

'As Bridget had been,' he answered dourly. 'I offered you the job here more to please your mother than for any other reason. I didn't think you'd take it and was a bit taken aback when you volunteered to come, especially after my behaviour with Birdie. But not even my rudeness seemed to put you off during the journey to Loch Lomond, although I half expected you to refuse to come any further. I think it was when I came back into the kitchen the night we arrived here that I began to realise that there was more to you than met my eye. Although you must have been tired and cold and hungry, and although I was in a filthy mood after being let down by the Andersons, you rose to the occasion, cooked an almost perfect meal and sang to yourself while you did it. I had a flash of insight of what life with you might be, and from then my due aim was to keep you here until the shock of Noll's death had worn off and you came alive again. I knew you wouldn't return my love until you were free of him. I could only go slowly hoping that time would heal and that then you'd notice that I was here. The phoney engagement helped a little to make you more aware of me, but unfortunately Gregor, who brought it about, became a regular visitor and I was afraid that he was going to reap the benefit of all my patient efforts.'

His face tautened and darkened when he spoke of Gregor and Gina had a glimpse of a passionate possessiveness which sent a strange little quiver of excitement through her.

'When I came in today and found your note,' continued Will tersely, 'I was furious, mostly with myself for having allowed you to get under my skin to such an extent that the thought of you going anywhere with Gregor made me feel murderous. I suppose I should be grateful to your kitten. If Gregor hadn't decided to rescue him you'd have left the glen before I returned from Ullapool. As it was I was very tempted to push Gregor down the rest of the cliff into the sea, instead of rescuing him.'

'Oh, you were jealous of him!' accused Gina, clapping her hands together, feeling rather pleased that she was capable of rousing such an intense emotion in such a self-contained man as Will.

'I admit it,' he ground out savagely. 'And Andrea didn't help at all when she brought your cases back here. For one thing she interrupted us at a rather special moment and for another, she told me that you were afraid to tell me that you preferred Gregor to me and wanted to discontinue our engagement. Are you in love with him, George? If so say so, and I'll take you over to the castle now.'

'Would I have said that I was ready to take the next step with you if I were in love with him, silly?' she retorted, smiling up at him, sensing suddenly that he was very uncertain and had been made so by his experience with Bridget. 'I love *you*, Will. Look!'

She held out her left hand to him and he glanced down at it. It was ringless.

'Where's Noll's ring?' he demanded, looking directly at her, his eyes darkening.

'I've decided not to wear it any more,' she replied, laughter bubbling up inside her. 'I've developed a liking for topazes because someone said once that they match my eyes. If I thought you'd give them to me I'd stay here for ever, even when the swans fly south, I'd stay with you, Will.'

'Then you shall have them, sweetheart,' he said, laughing with her, grasping her hands and drawing her towards him. Her fingers rested lightly for a moment on his chest and she felt passion stir and ripple through him, then she was swamped again by his embrace.

The lamp on the table flickered a little as if running short of oil, making black shadows dance on the walls of the room. From his basket, which was still scattered with playing cards, the kitten gazed drowsily at the closely entwined figures of the man and woman. When they turned and walked slowly from the room he was tempted to follow them and to go where they were going, but the day on the cliff had tired him and he was loath to move. Yawning widely, he circled round several times in the basket to make himself more comfortable, curled up and closed his eyes, content for once to stay alone in the kitchen for the night, and gradually the flame of the lamp died down and went out, leaving the room in darkness.

Golden Harlequin Library

A Treasury of Harlequin Romances!

Many of the all time favorite Harlequin Romance Novels have not been available, until now, since the original printing. But on this special introductory offer, they are yours in an exquisitely bound, rich gold hardcover with royal blue imprint. Three complete unabridged novels in each volume. And the cost is so very low you'll be amazed!

Handsome, Hardcover Library Editions at Paperback Prices! ONLY $1.95 each volume. or $11.70 the set

This very special collection of classic Harlequin Romances would be a distinctive addition to your library. And imagine what a delightful gift they'd make for any Harlequin reader!

Volumes 43 to 48 Just Published!
See following page.

GOLDEN
HARLEQUIN LIBRARY

$11.70
per set

Each volume contains 3 complete
Harlequin Romances

$1.95
each volume

To: Harlequin Reader Service, Dept. G 404
M.P.O. Box 707, Niagara Falls, N.Y. 14302
Canadian address: Stratford, Ont., Canada

☐ Please send me complete listing of the 48 Golden Harlequin
Library Volumes.

☐ Please send me the Golden Harlequin Library editions I
have indicated above.

I enclose $.................... (No C.O.D.'s) To help defray postage
and handling costs, please add 50c.

Name _____

Address _____

City/Town _____

State/Province ____ _____ Zip_____

G 404

FREE! Harlequin Romance Catalogue

Here is a wonderful opportunity to read many of the Harlequin Romances you may have missed.

The HARLEQUIN ROMANCE CATALOGUE lists hundreds of titles which possibly are no longer available at your local bookseller. To receive your copy, just fill out the coupon below, mail it to us, and we'll rush your catalogue to you!

Following this page you'll find a sampling of a few of the Harlequin Romances listed in the catalogue. Should you wish to order any of these immediately, kindly check the titles desired and mail with coupon.

Have You Missed Any of These
Harlequin Romances?